FLARE
of
PROMISE

(Asylums for Magical Threats #4)

Jessie Donovan

Flare of Promise
Copyright © 2016 Laura Hoak-Kagey
Mythical Lake Press, LLC
First Edition

Cover Art by Clarissa Yeo of Yocla Designs.

ISBN 13: 978-1942211389

To my AMT readers

Thank you for your patience in waiting for this story

Other Books by Jessie Donovan

Stonefire Dragons

Sacrificed to the Dragon
Seducing the Dragon
Revealing the Dragons
Healed by the Dragon
Reawakening the Dragon
Loved by the Dragon
Surrendering to the Dragon (May 2016)

Lochguard Highland Dragons

The Dragon's Dilemma
The Dragon Guardian
The Dragon's Heart (Summer 2016)

Asylums for Magical Threats

Blaze of Secrets
Frozen Desires
Shadow of Temptation
Flare of Promise

Cascade Shifters

Convincing the Cougar
Reclaiming the Wolf
Cougar's First Christmas
Resisting the Cougar

Chapter One

"*The spreading illness had finally reached a village a few hundred miles from where Loreley lived with her family, which meant it would soon be in her hometown. The humans didn't know the sickness was beyond the ability of their doctors; only magic could stop the life-taking curse currently killing off both humans and Feiru (FEY-roo) by the thousands.*

The only ones with strong enough magic to break the curse were called the Four Talents. The four legendary elemental magic users controlled the particles in the air. Together, they could battle the sickness and win. Yet as word spread of their unique powers, the humans tried everything in their power to capture the Talents to use as weapons in their own wars and petty arguments.

To succeed, the Four Talents needed an army to protect them. Those with special magical abilities that showed up later in life, such as Loreley's ability to control others with song, only appeared when the Four Talents needed help fighting off the sickness. No matter how difficult it might be to say goodbye to her family, Loreley's ability marked her as special. Some might see a latent ability as a curse, but Loreley viewed it as a gift. And not just any gift, but one that could help save the world."

—From the Legend of Loreley the Siren

JESSIE DONOVAN

Present Day
Sichuan Province, China

Petra Brandt lay on the ground next to Millie Ward, her friend-slash-sometimes-enemy, and watched the side of the mountain through her binoculars. After several days of surveillance, Petra knew there was a hidden door in the section of the rock she watched. And if a certain English scientist kept to the same schedule as he had for the last few days, he should be exiting the research facility housed inside the mountain in the next couple of minutes.

Despite the fact she'd seen Dr. William Evans every morning for the last few days, Petra still held her breath in anticipation. The shock of seeing her ex-fiancé might never wear off.

Get it together, Brandt. Think of not only Will's life, but also your brother's.

Right. Petra had spent the last two years working as a mercenary. She could handle watching the man she still loved and control any lingering feelings she might have for him. All that mattered was saving his life.

Sixty seconds later, the rock slid open and Petra raised her binoculars again. Dr. William Evans walked out in a grey t-shirt and black tracksuit pants. Once the door closed behind him, the man began a series of stretches. Each bend of his body or flex of his arms made her draw in a breath.

Petra had always found Will attractive. But over the years, he'd toned up. His broad shoulders and lean, muscled biceps made her want to run down the hill and jump into his arms.

But she couldn't. Will thought she was dead and Petra needed to keep it that way.

8

The woman at her side gave a low whistle and whispered, "Are you sure we need to do this today? I really could do with a few more days of watching that bloke stretch." Will moved into a lunge stretch, showcasing his ass. Millie continued, "Bloody hell. Look at that arse. Are you sure he's a scientist?"

Petra tightened her grip on her binoculars. If she didn't need Millie Ward's help, Petra would punch the woman in the face. "Yes, he is. Now, can you focus? You're up in less than five minutes."

"Oh, don't worry. If there's one thing I can do well, it's flirt with a man."

Lowering her binoculars, Petra looked to Millie. "You'd better do more than flirt if you wish to distract him enough for our plan."

Millie met her gaze and grinned. "Why, Petra, I never thought you'd allow me to sleep with him. You're such a generous friend."

"I'm not your friend," Petra growled out. "And stick to the plan or I'll put in a call to Larsen."

At the mention of Millie's former captor, her grin faded and she frowned. "That threat is getting old, Petra. One of these times I'm going to test the threat and you'll falter." She lowered her voice. "I know you're starting to enjoy my company."

Until last week, Petra and Millie had known of each other, but hadn't ever worked together. They both worked private security or mercenary gigs. The unwritten rule was to stay clear of a fellow mercenary unless they stood in the way of a target. A few times, Millie and Petra had had to trick each other to finish their jobs and collect their fees, but that was it.

Then Petra had learned about the threat to Will's life and had needed help. Her twin brother worked for a dangerous man and Petra couldn't risk her brother's boss finding out about Will. After all, that boss was a mean bastard who wouldn't think twice of using a weakness such as a former fiancé to get what he wanted. Eventually, Petra would take care of the asshole Sean Reilly. But not until she knew Will was safe.

After all, she'd faked her own death two years earlier to protect Will. Petra wasn't about to waste that heartbreak by allowing Will to die now.

Narrowing her eyes at Millie, Petra finally replied, "Whether I like you or not is irrelevant. Complete this mission and I'll be in your debt. Fuck up and I'll deliver you to Larsen myself. Hell, I might even take you to his boss, Giovanni Sinclair."

At the mention of Giovanni, Millie's face turned expressionless. "I'll do my part, but you really need to learn to lighten up, Petra. Your level of seriousness is bound to bring on a heart attack by the time you're forty."

Petra checked her watch and motioned for Millie to go. "You're on."

Tossing her dark blonde hair over her shoulder, Millie fluttered her eyes. "I'll try my best."

"Just remember the scientific jargon I gave you and you'll do fine. He needs to believe you work in the AMT research facility."

AMT stood for the Asylums for Magical Threats, which was essentially a prison system for first-born magic users. Humans didn't know of the existence of the *Feiru,* and the AMT Oversight Committee did everything in its power to keep it that way, including taking away twelve and thirteen-year-old children from their parents right before their magic matured and became dangerous.

FLARE OF PROMISE

Millie inched toward the closest bush. "I've pretended to be a genetic researcher for a previous assignment. This is similar. I'll be fine."

Petra's curiosity wondered what job had required Millie Ward to play that part. But there wasn't time to ask. "Just go. If you don't leave now, he'll jog out of your reach and we'll have to wait until tomorrow. By then, who knows if someone will have noticed our presence."

"Fine, fine." Millie stood up behind the bush and tapped her ear. "Just let me know the second you spot trouble."

"Just don't go inside the mountain or your earpiece will stop working."

Millie muttered something Petra only picked up through the two-way radio earpiece. "I'm not a rookie."

Before Petra could say anything, Millie made her way down the hill to the exercise path used by the researchers and guards from the AMT facility. There was only a small section of the trail that wasn't monitored by security cameras thanks to various trees and bushes blocking the shot.

Raising her binoculars again, Petra willed for everything to go perfectly. They had one chance and one chance only to get this operation right. She refused to think about what would happen if they failed.

~ ~ ~

William Evans jogged at a steady rhythm. The soft falls of his feet, combined with his breathing, helped his brain to focus.

His own volunteer research subjects would be arriving shortly. The three *Feiru* had developed magical abilities in the last few weeks. Unlike first-born *Feiru*, whom controlled either wind, water, earth, or fire magic, the late developers had a mishmash of powers that he'd never heard of before. One man could sometimes change the weather with words; a woman had the ability to shift into a fiery bird and direct other animals; and the second woman could control others with song.

He couldn't wait to start his research and find a way to eradicate the mysterious latent abilities. Doing so would help protect the *Feiru* from the humans, of whom only a few knew of their existence.

Of course, Will's motives weren't entirely altruistic. He stared down at his hand and imagined holding someone else's, one with a red slash across the palm. The second he changed the image to one of skin free of injury, his hand glowed a faint green.

Clenching his fingers, he banished the image and pumped his legs harder. *I'm sorry, Leyna. I will still find a way to eradicate elemental magic so that no one else can kill unnecessarily again. But to do that, I need to banish my own power. Otherwise, they'll lock me up and I can't help anyone.*

As always, silence was his answer.

Mentally speaking with his dead fiancée helped Will more than he would like to admit. Nothing he did would ever bring her back, but he would ensure that no one else would be burned alive simply because a rogue first-born elemental fire user had been careless.

Every day for the last two years he had wondered what his life would be like if he'd only agreed to meet Leyna for dinner that night. Instead, he'd been so focused on the research for his doctoral thesis that he'd missed all of her calls and text messages. Leyna had gone out alone and been accosted by a drunk fire user in a small park in London.

As he always did when he thought of Leyna's death, Will's drive to succeed pumped harder. He would find a way to rid the world of magic if it was the last thing he did. Leyna's death would have a purpose. He'd make sure of it.

He focused on reviewing his current research and hypothesis and ran on autopilot. So much so, that when he turned a corner, he nearly ran chest first into a young woman with dark blonde hair and green eyes.

While he didn't collide with her, the woman did grab onto his arm to keep from falling over. She cried out in pain and raised one of her feet off the ground. Will lowered his head and met the woman's eye. "Are you okay? I'm sorry. I didn't know anyone else used the path at this time of day."

The woman inhaled deeply and gave a weak smile. "This is my first attempt at jogging and I think the universe is telling me to give it up."

The woman's accent was from the North of England. "If you let one mishap derail you from your task, then you aren't going to get very far."

She bobbed her head. "You're right, of course. It's just that I'm new here and everything is strange. I've never been to China before this and it's been a bit of a shock. You sound as if you're from somewhere near London, so you probably understand what I mean."

The woman hopped on one foot and he mentally cursed. At this rate, he wasn't going to finish his run before his subjects arrived. "May I help you back inside, Miss...?"

"I'm Donna Dixon. And you are?"

"I'm Dr. Evans."

Donna blinked her eyes quickly; flutter might be a more appropriate word. Bloody hell, was she flirting with him? The woman purred, "Do we really need to be so formal?"

"I don't think I've seen you before. What department did you work in again?"

Irritation flashed in Donna's eyes. Good. Maybe she'd take the hint. Will had zero interest in romantic entanglements. His own freedom depended on the success of his research.

Leaning on his arm for support, Donna answered, "I'm a genetic research assistant."

Will was careful to keep the disdain from his voice. "For the children?"

"Yes, of course."

While Will's work focused on adults with latent magical abilities, the Sichuan research facility had a much bigger secret. The children born inside the AMT compounds to inmates were shipped to China at a young age. A team of scientists studied them for genetic shifts because of the experiments conducted on their mothers. It was all part of the AMT Oversight Committee's bigger goal to eradicate magic.

However, Will didn't agree with hiding the children away from the world, especially for the innocents born without magic.

Still, he couldn't afford to alienate the other research staff. His own boss, Giovanni Sinclair, had bigger plans that required their cooperation.

Wanting to rid himself of the woman's company, he placed an arm around her shoulders and maneuvered them back toward the entrance. "I'll help you inside. But after that, I really must go back to my lab."

"I'd love to see your lab. I don't think you're in the same department as me and it'd be fascinating to see what you're up to."

He glanced down at Donna. His gut told him something was off about the woman. "What level clearance do you have?"

She answered without missing a beat, "Seven."

The highest level was five.

Will stopped and swung the woman around until he had her shoulders pinned with one arm and his thumb at her carotid artery with the other. "Who are you and what do you want?"

The woman murmured, "I'm sorry about this," before she elbowed him in the stomach and knocked the wind out of him.

Donna tried to sweep his foot to knock him off balance. Since Will had spent the last two years training against any sort of attack, he moved his leg out of the way and tightened his arm around the woman's throat. She elbowed him again and he grunted. But there was no way she was going to win. Another few seconds of pressure against her artery and the woman would fall unconscious.

He couldn't wait to find out who she was and why the hell she was lying about working at the research facility.

Of course, the bigger question was why someone was targeting Will at all. His abilities were a secret, or so he thought.

~~~

Petra cursed as Millie and Will tried to disarm each other. From the look of things, Will was winning.

She could either show her face and use Will's reaction to knock him unconscious or she'd have to chance shooting a tranquilizer dart from her current position.

15

Given that she was at least 400 feet from Will and Millie, only luck would guarantee the shot with the equipment she'd brought with her.

Tossing her binoculars to the side, Petra spoke so Millie could hear her through the earpiece. "I'm coming, Millie. Find a way to stay conscious a little longer."

As she took off down the hill toward the exercise path, Petra took out her Taser. The tranquilizer would knock Will out for far too long. The last thing she needed was for his absence to be noted. Yes, she wanted to rescue him, but she also needed time to escape.

Pumping her legs as fast as she could, she drew near where Will and Millie were having their altercation. Millie had snaked an arm behind her and Petra watched as she grabbed Will's balls and twisted.

Even as Will cried out in pain and loosened his grip, jealousy shot through Petra's body. She had no claim on Will Evans, but she didn't like any other woman's hands on him.

What the hell am I thinking? Pushing aside her jealousy, she charged at Will's back and shouted, "Now!"

Millie released her hold and rolled off to the side. Will turned his head and met her eyes right before she shot the Taser cartridge at his back. Even as his body shook, he managed, "Leyna?"

Two seconds later, he was unconscious on the ground.

Kneeling down, Petra lightly brushed Will's forehead. He wouldn't be out for long. As soon as he regained consciousness, Petra would have to act as if she didn't care about him.

Yet as she touched his warm skin, a longing she'd buried deep inside broke free. Despite all of the time that had passed and the drastic changes in her life, Petra still wanted him. More than that, a small part of her wanted to drop the persona of Petra Brandt and become Leyna Grunwald again. That life had been so much simpler.

Her eyes fell on his lips. She wanted to kiss him more than anything she'd wanted in years. Surely she had enough time to give the good-bye kiss she'd never had a chance to give.

Before she could lean down more than an inch, Millie's hushed voice stopped her. "I know he's attractive and all, but you'll have to save your snogging for later."

Millie was right. Saving Will's life was far more important than walking down memory lane. Petra leaned away from Will and ignored the pain in her heart. After all, the distance between them only existed to protect Will. "We're going to have to adjust the plan."

Millie shrugged. "Fine by me. Although, if you expect me to carry him, you're going to be in for a surprise. That man is pure muscle."

Petra growled. "Stop admiring his body."

Her partner studied Petra a second before motioning toward Will. "Then what do you want to do? If we take his ID card, he'll alert the guards and they'll probably void it."

Petra opened one of the pockets of her cargo pants and took out a small pad of paper and a mini-pencil. "I'll leave him a note."

"Right, because he's just going to go along with what you say."

Jotting down her message, Petra murmured, "He will."

"Why?"

She folded the note and tucked it into Will's palm. She met Millie's eyes. "Because at one point, he was going to marry me."

CHAPTER TWO

Will groaned as his brain started to work again. Someone had tased him, but the details were fuzzy.

When he finally opened his eyes, he looked around at the empty exercise path and it all came back to him. Donna was gone, as was the ghost of his Leyna.

It had to have been his imagination. He'd attended Leyna's funeral. Sure, she'd been cremated, but his sweet Leyna never would've tried to fake her own death.

Yet remembering the hard eyes and weapons strapped to Leyna's ghost made him wonder if it really had been her.

Not that he had time to think about it. The sun's position told him his volunteers would be arriving shortly.

Little by little, Will forced his muscles to work again. When he reached his hands, they closed on to something firm, yet malleable. With effort, he raised his hand and saw a piece of paper tucked in his palm.

A minute later, he sat up and unfolded the note. Inside was the handwriting of a dead woman:

Meet me at the local expat restaurant this evening. Come alone and I'll explain everything.
~Leyna
PS—Proof that I am who I say: Derwentwater, push, love.

His heart skipped a beat. Derwentwater in the Lake District was the place where Leyna had not only accidentally pushed him into the lake, it had also been where he'd said he'd loved her for the first time.

Running a hand through his hair, he scanned the surroundings. While someone could've researched his past or talked to his brother to find out about the events at Derwentwater in Keswick, seeing Leyna's face was too much of a coincidence. What if she were still alive? He could be angry with her for lying later. He needed to see the woman and determine her identity.

But he couldn't do any of that if he missed welcoming his test subjects. Will's freedom was controlled by Giovanni Sinclair. He couldn't risk upsetting his boss.

Slowly rising to his feet, Will tucked the note into his pocket. As he tamped down the small flicker of hope in his chest, Will schooled his face into a neutral expression. He couldn't allow anyone to find out he'd been accosted by two women during his run. Considering the two women had chosen the only blind spot he'd noticed along the path, they had to be professionals.

The question was why did they need him? And moreover, if it truly was Leyna he'd spotted earlier, why had she waited until now to show her face?

His earlier enthusiasm about starting his new research faded. As he scanned the surrounding hills, Will knew he would constantly be thinking of the upcoming meeting at the restaurant. The trick would be in acting as if everything was normal. Not only was Giovanni observant, the head warden of the facility—Liang—was more so.

The only good thing was Will had ten hours to think of an excuse to visit the local restaurant. During that time, he'd also tuck away any lingering feelings he still possessed for Leyna. For all he knew, the mysterious woman wanted to use his past against

19

him. If she thought Will was an easy target, she was in for a big surprise.

~~~

The instant Petra and Millie were inside the abandoned house they used as a base, Millie turned on Petra. "How could you keep this from me? Partners don't keep secrets that could cost them their lives."

Petra sighed. "Stop being overdramatic. My connection to Will had no impact on the mission. When it became relevant, I told you."

Crossing her arms over her chest, Millie raised her brows. "Too right it's become bloody relevant. Tell me what happened or I'll risk Larsen, Sinclair, and the lot by running away."

The only person who knew about Petra's real identity was her brother, Dominick, and for good reason. Not just because they'd both changed identities together, but also because when someone worked as a mercenary, enemies always looked for weaknesses. Former friends and lovers were at the top of the list of targets.

Yet as she studied Millie Ward, Petra didn't think the woman would sell her information to the highest bidder. After all, Petra knew of Millie's involvement in trying to free the first-born magic users. That information could be useful to the right people. In a way, they were at an impasse until trust developed. "It's not overly complicated. My brother got into some trouble and needed my help. To protect Will, I faked my death and created a new persona."

"You can act all indifferent now but I saw the way you brushed his forehead. Hell, you were about to kiss him."

Petra kept her expression neutral. "A momentary lapse that won't happen again, I assure you."

"Right, and the sky is turning green."

Petra growled. "Drop it, Millie. You know enough to complete the mission. Don't expect any more."

Millie continued as if Petra hadn't spoken. "You know what I think? I suspect you go back and forth about your choice every day. But was it worth it? Finding love isn't easy. If I did, I'd never toss it away."

Petra debated walking away. But if Millie was to be her back-up for her meeting later on, she needed to keep the woman on her side. Petra raised her brows. "Oh, really? You have two brothers. Imagine if one of their lives depended on your help. I bet you would've done the same."

"I don't like hypotheticals. But that scientist bloke doesn't look like the type to marry a mercenary. I have a feeling you did a hell of a lot more than fake your death to help your brother."

Millie was right, but Petra wasn't about to tell her. "Look, the other details of my past are irrelevant. We need to prepare for tonight. While I don't think he will turn me in, there's always a small chance Will's changed as much as me and we need to be ready."

"One last question and I'll hold off until at least after this meeting. Deal?"

"Fine."

Millie tilted her head. "Someone's grumpy." Petra opened her mouth but Millie beat her to the reply. "Why did he call you Leyna?"

Petra didn't hesitate. "Because when I faked my death, I changed my name. It's Self-Preservation 101. Now that your questions will cease, let's both figure out a number of escape routes."

Millie replied, "Why not just kidnap him? I'm sure we could find somewhere for you two to run off together. Then you'd both be safe and you could enjoy life a bit more." Millie flicked her hand to Petra. "You're far too tense. A little sex could go a long way toward relaxing you."

Petra had considered going with Will, but had decided against it. "His current position is powerful. According to both of our contacts, his boss is Giovanni Sinclair. We definitely don't need his adopted father—the uncle dearest of your brother's girlfriend, by the way—getting wind of Will's disappearance. Remember, he has his own strange power and James Sinclair is out to rid the world of all magic."

"Don't remind me," Millie muttered before raising her voice back to normal levels. "But you want Will to disappear, remember? That's our entire reason for being here, unless you've changed your plan without telling me."

Petra shook her head. "No, the plan is to make Will disappear on his own. It's far easier for him to blend in and create a new identity without me since I've made more than a few enemies over the years."

Millie rolled her eyes. "I believe you think you're more badass than you actually are."

"Millie," Petra growled.

"Fine, fine. But back to tonight. The AMT research facility usually sends out bodyguards to watch over their employees. Do you think a bodyguard will follow Will around tonight, too? Or is he stealthy enough to lose a tail? Since he hasn't left the facility since we've been here, apart from his runs, I worry about unexpected surprises."

She nodded. "He'll probably have a guard. But that's where you come in. You're pretty good at fluttering your eyelashes. I'm sure you won't mind doing that again tonight to distract them."

Placing her hands on her hips, Millie raised her chin. "I may be gorgeous, but I have a brain, too. I never would've gotten this far without it."

"Are we really going down this road again? Yes, you're good at your job. But out of the two of us, who has the greatest chance of convincing Will to trust us?"

"I suspect this Leyna person. Who was she again?"

Shaking her head, Petra motioned toward the hallway. "Just help get things ready for tonight. We'll reconvene two hours before. In the meantime, I have some people to contact."

Millie rolled her eyes. "Right, like all of those ones who turned down helping you with this assignment?"

Petra gritted her teeth and forced her voice to be even. "I did manage to get some help with regards to weapons and a place to stay, but I'm not going to argue with you any more. Leave before I take out some of my pent-up energy by punching you in the face."

"As if you could best me."

"You said that about Will, and he just about had you unconscious."

Millie sniffed. "I had things under control."

Petra massaged her temples. "You're nearly as bad as my brother."

"I'd say the same about one of mine, except he's mellowed out a lot since finding love. Maybe you should try the same."

"Yes, because a woman with dangerous enemies is quite the catch." She waved toward the door again. "I need a break from you to regroup. Go."

Studying her a second, Millie nodded. "I'll check in with you in a few hours."

As soon as she heard Millie's door close, Petra let out a sigh and placed her head in her hands. Not because of Millie, although the woman tried her patience, but because Petra had exactly nine hours to contain her feelings about Will.

Despite her display of nonchalance with Millie, seeing Will again was going to be difficult. She couldn't risk showing any sign of affection because she had a feeling that if she did, Will might try to pursue her.

Not because he felt the same way about her as she did him, but Will would want answers. Once he put his mind to finding them, he didn't give up. The man had always been as stubborn as an ox. And given his new position, he might even have the resources and contacts necessary to find her later if he tried.

Rubbing her face, Petra inhaled deeply. *Right.* She could do this. All she had to do was save the man she still loved and then hurt him so badly he'd want nothing to do with her ever again. That couldn't be that difficult, right?

If that were so, then why did her heart ache at the thought of never seeing William Evans again? Petra was starting to understand why people hired mercenaries to take care of a problem within a family. Attachments, no matter how well bottled up, made things fucking difficult.

~~~

Will had just managed to don his white coat and boot up his computer before Gio walked into his lab. Even though Will had seen the man's face a hundred times before over the last few weeks, this time Will noticed something different. Gio's usually calm and collected face was replaced with a clenched jaw and narrowed eyes. Will asked, "Did you talk with your father?"

Gio took a deep inhalation and let out his breath. "Yes. He wanted to take away my high-level clearance."

Will couldn't care less about Gio's relations with his adopted father. But Gio was the reason Will had his freedom, so he needed to ensure nothing went wrong. "Why?"

"Because Liang told my father I've spent too much time in the children's research wing."

Will shrugged. Liang was the director of the research facility in Sichuan. "You have spent too much time there. I told you to be cautious."

Gio motioned with his hands about the room, asking if it was safe to talk. Since Will had neutralized the bugs, he nodded and Gio continued, "You know what they're doing is illegal. Keeping first-borns locked up to protect both themselves and the public is one thing. But keeping children with no magical powers in prison and denying them an education, that's criminal."

"Spoken like a true future politician."

"Stop it, Evans. I will find a way into the British Parliament and once I'm there, I'll ensure the safety of humans and *Feiru* without violating the law."

If given the chance, Gio would carry on about the future of *Feiru*-kind for an hour. Glancing to the clock, Evans changed the topic. "The volunteer test subjects are still coming, right?"

"Yes, they'll be here momentarily. Although you want to make sure you don't fuck this up, Evans."

Will narrowed his eyes. "Don't ever question my abilities as a researcher. If anyone will screw things up, it's you. Stop asking so many bloody questions. Leave that to me."

Gio's voice was calm and steely as he replied, "Remember your place. One word from me to the scientists here about your strange, healing light and they'll lock you up in one of the cells."

"Threaten me if you wish, but you need me."

Gio raised an eyebrow. "You need me as well. I did learn something from my father that may interest you."

"And that is?"

"If we progress well and you can provide evidence as to what is causing these latent abilities, you might be able to work with the team studying E-1655."

E-1655 was the serial number assigned to an elemental earth first-born female. Unlike most first-born *Feiru* who needed to point their hands to a particular compass direction to use their abilities, E-1655 could manipulate the earth regardless of where her hands were placed. "Is she still drugged in a semi-stupor in Hong Kong?"

Gio shook his head. "They've actually moved her to a secret location I don't even know about. But they keep losing researchers any time they stop the drugs and allow the woman to regain full consciousness. Her magic is dangerous and she's injuring people left and right."

Will had spent the last two years looking for ways to eradicate elemental magic; E-1655 could be the key he needed to do it. "Has the woman given birth?"

"Not yet. They're afraid to sterilize her. Some think it may affect her unusual abilities."

Each first-born *Feiru* was assigned to an experiment track at the age of thirteen inside the AMT compounds. The mental, breeding, and gene therapy experiments had never sat well with Will. He preferred willing volunteers, not coerced ones. "I may be interested, provided we can solve the little problem of latent abilities first."

"Good." Gio's mobile phone beeped with a text message. After reading it, Gio glanced up again. "They're here."

A flicker of anticipation flared in Will's stomach. "Right, then let's get started."

Gio exited the room to greet the volunteers and Will followed. Talking about the future with Gio had temporarily helped Will forget about Leyna's note. Hopefully his work would make time move quickly. Clutching the wad of paper in his pocket, the urge to run out of the building and search for the woman from earlier coursed through his body.

A small voice in the back of his head brought up the fact that if Leyna was still alive, Will's entire reason for living over the last two years would become moot.

But he'd cross that bridge when he came to it. Entering the main security office, Will nodded to the guards standing over three unconscious bodies in wheelchairs. One of the guards spoke up in perfect English. "They should be out for another thirty minutes."

Will answered, "Right, then follow me. We need to secure them in their special quarters before they wake up."

As he led the guards back toward his lab, Will glanced behind him at the two women and one man in the wheelchairs. For a split second, he wondered what their stories were. Did they have families? Had they been blackmailed into coming here? Where had they been before developing their strange abilities?

Then he remembered he might lose his freedom if he started to care. Much like he'd done for the past two years, Will pushed his emotions deep down and focused on the theories he needed to prove.

CHAPTER THREE

Petra pretended to stare at her cell phone, but in reality, she kept an eye on the surrounding patrons of the restaurant where she was meeting Will. The room was on the small side, but clean and filled with about fifteen tables, plus a bar up front.

The local humans believed the AMT research facility was actually a British pharmaceutical company and their economy had developed around it. The restaurant Petra had chosen catered to foreigners, which meant German-born Petra fit right in. A few other *Feiru* and one human backpacker also filled the room.

Keeping her voice low, Petra murmured, "Update?"

Millie answered through the earpiece. "There is a large group of non-Chinese heading right this way. I can't tell if Will's in the group or not. But don't worry, I have your back. I'm willing to undo a few buttons on my blouse and reveal the girls to distract the men if you need it."

Only because she was sitting alone at the table did Petra not roll her eyes and give a rather colorful reply.

With nothing to do but scroll around on her phone to look as if she were reading something, Petra's heart beat faster in anticipation of seeing Will.

Her life had changed a lot over the past two years and she wondered if Will would even recognize the woman she'd once been.

FLARE OF PROMISE

After giving up the pursuit of her PhD in chemistry, Petra had spent months learning hand-to-hand combat and self-defense. Her life had been safe in the beginning only because of her ability to cook meth. But she'd never trusted the drug lord who'd convinced her brother Dom to join his ranks. Not only had her martial arts skills saved their lives later, the discipline of daily practice had also helped Petra focus on her new life and forget about Will Evans.

Truth be told, Millie wouldn't recognize the woman known as Leyna but now Petra. Leyna had loved to tease, scream at the sight of a spider, and had had a weakness for white chocolate. But Petra had to be strong, strategic, and clever. Gone were the weaknesses and easygoing nature, and in its place, she had developed a hardened persona.

The only question was whether Petra could retain her new persona while talking with Will or not.

Get a grip, Brandt. You've taken down powerful men and women. Surely you can handle one random scientist.

Nodding to herself, Petra looked up at the sound of people entering the front door. At the front of the small crowd stood Will with his strong jaw and close-cut beard. When he finally met her eyes, Will blinked.

Hoping to fool the other patrons, Petra smiled and tilted her head in invitation. Millie had sworn earlier that the head tilt, when combined with a revealing shirt and a suggestive smile, always worked to bring a man over.

Since Petra lacked Millie's confidence, she barely restrained herself from tucking her hair behind her ears. Will had known her originally with short hair. Would he like her hair longer?

Stop it. For both her safety and Will's, they could never be together. The sooner Petra remembered that, the better.

29

Yet as Will walked toward her table, her heart pounded. She'd dreamed of the normalcy of going on a date with Will hundreds, if not thousands of times over the years. She may never be able to kiss him again, but she sure as hell could drink in his face and memorize it for the future.

Whether she liked it or not, Petra would probably love William Evans to the day she died. However, his life was more important than her desires. To save him, she would need to drive him away.

But, damn, it was going to hurt.

~~~

Will blinked at the sight of Leyna wearing a deep blue top that was cut low to reveal the tops of her breasts. Her light brown hair was longer than he'd ever seen it, but he loved the way it framed her face to make her green eyes pop. God, her eyes. He may have doubted the woman at first, but even from about six feet away, the eyes told him his beloved Leyna was still alive.

And he was determined to find out why.

He approached the table. Pulling out a chair, he slid in and kept his voice low. "Start talking."

She raised an eyebrow. "So much for hello."

Will glanced from the corner of his eyes, but all of his colleagues were busy talking amongst themselves. Since he'd told them he'd had a date with a new assistant, they wouldn't question him having dinner with a beautiful woman.

Clenching his knee under the table, he pushed that thought aside and focused on the grief and pain he'd suffered. "At least you're still smiling. We're on a date, love. So keep up the facade."

Leyna purred, "Oh, I can keep up an act as long as necessary."

30

"So is that what I was, then? Part of an act?"

Regret flashed in Leyna's eyes. But it was gone before he could blink. "Of course not. But I'm not here to talk about the past. I'm trying to give you a future."

Will raised an eyebrow. "Why now? You had no problem keeping quiet for two years."

She answered in a low whisper. "Because I couldn't stand the thought of you being locked away and used as a guinea pig."

He almost believed the sincerity in her voice. Then he remembered the days after her death, filled with crying, shouting out in anger at anyone who tried to console him, and the self-imposed isolation. It had been pure hell.

If Leyna had cared for him at all, she would've sought him out earlier. The woman he'd loved back then would've cared about easing his pain instead of causing it.

Yet despite the memories of hurt and betrayal, a small part of him still wanted the truth.

To ensure no one overheard, Will moved his chair next to Leyna's. Yet as soon as he did, her soft, feminine scent filled his nose. Despite the years between them, Leyna still smelled lightly of vanilla. He'd always told her it made him want to eat her up. Back then, she'd even blushed whenever he'd said it.

However, eyeing the current, hard woman next to him, he doubted this version of Leyna ever blushed. Hell, he was surprised she still had a heart.

Leaning down to her ear, the vanilla scent was stronger and he battled the urge to take a deep inhalation. If that wasn't a big enough temptation, her warm cheek was right in front of him. Her skin had been quite soft back in the day. He itched to trace her cheek and find out if it were the same.

He might be angry at her lies, but he'd be a fool to deny his lingering attraction.

31

Get control of yourself, Evans. Clearing his throat, he finally murmured, "I don't know what you're talking about."

Leyna turned her head to meet his eyes. She still had gold flecks around the pupils.

He swore she drew in a breath, but her eyes remained neutral. "You know exactly what I'm talking about." She reached under the table and took his hand. The light brush of her fingers against his skin released a flood of desire. "Your hands are capable of so many things."

Bloody hell. She knew. "How?"

Tilting her head, her hair brushed the tops of her breasts. "Let's just say I'm resourceful."

"That isn't a proper answer."

She darted her eyes around the room. "I won't risk saying anything more here."

Will wanted to roar in frustration. But then he had an idea of how they could leave and talk alone. "Then there's only one thing to do."

Cupping her cheek, Will kissed her.

~~~

Petra had been so distracted by Will's heat and strong jaw that she hadn't predicted the kiss.

Yet as his lips moved against hers, she couldn't bring herself to push him away. If nothing else, the kiss would cement their act of being on a date. Her cover ID required everyone to believe that. She couldn't risk the mission.

Opening her mouth, she accepted his tongue with a moan.

Will's strokes took on a sense of urgency, as if he were making up for lost time. Petra tried to hold back so as not to encourage him beyond what was necessary, but when he nipped her lip, her life as Petra Brandt vanished and she became Leyna Grunwald once again.

And the memories of Leyna wanted more.

Threading her fingers through his hair, Petra pressed closer to him. Will stroked, and she pushed back. They each battled for control with their tongues. *Damn.* Will had always been a good kisser, but the last two years had made him more demanding and possessive. A small part of her wondered what he'd do if they were both naked and in bed. Being at Will's mercy sent a rush of wetness between her thighs.

Maybe her cover ID needed a hook-up to be convincing. One last night with Will might be necessary.

Yes, necessary. Not because she wanted to feel his warm hands cover her breasts as he took her from behind. No, because she didn't want to give anyone the idea she was anything other than a one-night stand.

All too soon, Will broke the kiss and she cried out. The corner of the bastard's mouth ticked up at the sound.

Petra might have just been manipulated. Taking a deep breath, she ignored the throbbing between her legs. Two could play at this game. Petra would turn the situation back into her favor.

As she stared into his eyes, she noted Will breathing as heavily as she was. Curiosity urged her to move a hand up his thigh to his groin and see if Will was as affected as she was.

Clenching her fingers, Petra's rational side won out and she kept her hand in place. She merely asked, "Why did you stop?"

He leaned to her ear again. "I just needed to convince my colleagues that I want to take you somewhere and bed you."

She resisted a frown. She had been right. "It was just a farce?"

"Of course. Provided you hang all over me as we leave, no one will think we're doing anything but rushing somewhere to get naked. That way, we can find a place to talk in private."

Disappointment flooded her body. It was irrational given she'd stomped on his heart by faking her death. She deserved him using her. But deep down, she'd always held on to the hope that if Will knew the reasons behind her actions, he would forgive her.

It might be too late for forgiveness.

Millie's voice whispered into her ear via the transmitter. "I knew you weren't as calm and collected as you made yourself out to be."

A quick glance and Petra spotted Millie at the bar, nursing a glass of wine. Will had made Petra forget Millie could hear everything she was saying via the earpiece.

Ignoring her partner in crime, Petra whispered to Will, "Okay, then let's get this show on the road. The sooner we're alone, the sooner I can tell you everything, get you on the path to safety, and leave town."

Rather than answer, Will placed a hand on the back of her neck and he nuzzled her cheek with his own. "Just make sure to play the part convincingly. A staff member is watching my every move."

"Oh, I'm a pretty good actor these days." Petra, ran a hand up Will's chest and his muscles tensed under her palm. "You'll see." She lightly nipped his neck before licking the sting. "Ready?"

Will cleared his throat and wrapped an arm around her shoulders. "Let's go."

They both stood and Petra leaned against Will's side, rubbing her hands over his chest and down to the fly of his jeans. Running a finger underneath the waistband, she brushed the head of his hard cock with her finger. Even though she only touched him through the material of his boxers, the memory of what he could do with all of those inches flashed inside her mind.

Holy crap. Control yourself, Brandt. True, she hadn't slept with anyone since Will. Merely kissing another guy had felt like a betrayal. But she wasn't about to fuck up her mission and risk Millie's safety because of her pent-up horniness. She could tease Will to get him to cooperate, unless circumstances forced her to sleep with him, which was always a possibility.

The second they hit the cool evening air, Will tugged her down the street and she whispered, "If we need to lose a tail, leave it to me."

Will looked over at her and merely shook his head. Whether because he thought they might have someone following them or for some other reason, he remained quiet. The silence gave her an opportunity to go through several mind-calming exercises. She would need all of the control she could muster if she was to spend any length of time alone with Will Evans and leave him behind at the end of her mission.

~ ~ ~

Since all the employees of the AMT research facilities lived inside the mountains in one of two employee wings, Will couldn't take Leyna to his quarters. Instead, he was taking Leyna to a hotel recommended by one of the other male staff members. Given its reputation as a hotspot for hook-ups, he was counting on the man following him to stay outside the hotel and not barge into their room.

Although after their kiss and Leyna's finger brushing his cock, Will was having a hell of a time concentrating on anything but his straining dick. The woman had lied to him and broken his heart. He shouldn't ache for her kisses or the light caress of her

35

fingers. Yet every time she touched him, it brought back the happy years they'd spent together.

He remembered the first time he'd seen her. They'd both been new graduate students at University College London. Another classmate had invited him to a small study group. However, that classmate had had a family emergency and the study group had ended up being only Will and Leyna. As they'd started talking, the hours had flown by. Not much studying had been done, but he'd managed to coax a date out of the sweet woman with a sharp wit and ability to laugh at herself.

Glancing at Leyna's profile at his side, he decided that woman was gone. His Leyna never would've lied to him. No, she would've talked with him and together they would've found a solution to stay together.

Maybe their time together had all been an act.

Will would listen to what Leyna had to say and then wash his hands of her. Otherwise, he'd never finish his important work and discover where *Feiru* latent abilities came from. Said abilities were a risk to the safety of the entire *Feiru* race because of their unpredictability. Not even the human agency tasked with keeping the *Feiru's* existence a secret, the *Feiru* Liaison Office, would be able to cover up thousands of new abilities popping up around the globe.

There was also the issue of Will's freedom.

His determination renewed, he turned down the final street and tugged Leyna into the hotel.

At the front desk, he pulled her against his side as he paid for a room. The whole time, Leyna's hands roamed his chest and back, sending waves of fire and electricity through his body.

The bloody woman played her role a little too well.

Will clenched his jaw to keep from outwardly reacting. Each brush of the blasted woman's finger turned his cock harder, but he'd be damned to let his face flush or breathing quicken.

Somehow, he managed to finish paying for a room without tugging Leyna close and kissing her again. As they made their way down the hall, every step he took only heightened his awareness of her heat at his side. He also noticed Leyna's soft curves had been replaced with toned muscle. Glancing down at her, he wondered what her daily life looked like these days.

They reached their room and Will unlocked the door. The second he and Leyna stepped inside, he swung her around and pinned her to the door with her arms over her head. "Start talking."

Leyna merely raised her chin. "Not until I know we're safe."

Will growled. "No one could know we'd be in this room at this moment. I think you're stalling."

Her eyes flashed. "Let me go or I will make you let me go."

He leaned down closer to her face. "Then try. We've both changed and I may have a surprise or two of my own."

"So do I."

She moved to kick him in the crotch, but Will stepped to the side and turned Leyna to face the door. With her hands behind her back, he used his body weight to keep her pinned in place. "You're going to have to do better than that."

Wiggling her arse against his groin, Will bit his lip to keep from making a noise. His head might not want to react to Leyna's touch, but his traitorous dick didn't care and begged for more friction. She wiggled again and a small groan escaped Will's lips.

Leyna's voice was husky as she whispered, "At least your body still wants me."

He gritted out, "Good thing my mind is stronger."

37

She moved her hips in a slow circle. "Is that so?" She moved again. "Then me telling you how wet and swollen I am for your cock won't affect you at all?"

Suddenly, all he could think about was stripping Leyna and pounding into her from behind. "Stop it."

"Why?" she purred. "Your body tells me what your mind doesn't. Fuck me, Will. I'm burning for you."

The rational side of his brain knew Leyna's words and actions were probably a trick. Yet as desire pounded through his body, he knew nothing would get done until he was naked and inside her. He would finally be able to say good-bye to the woman who'd broken his heart.

Lightly tugging her hair, he murmured, "Don't expect me to make love. I'm going to fuck you once as a good-bye. Then we're going to talk."

He tugged again and Leyna moaned. "Will."

"I'm going to let you go and give you thirty seconds to undress. Do it, and I'll take you. Try to pull something and I won't be so gentle next time. Understand?"

"You were never this alpha before."

He nibbled her earlobe before answering, "Sex first and talk later. Nod if you understand."

For a split second, Will thought Leyna was going to say no. Then she gave a curt nod and he smiled. "Good." He stepped back. "Thirty seconds, Leyna. Starting now."

~~~

Petra's original plan of distracting Will with her body had backfired. What had been one butt wiggle had turned into a dangerous game of desire and lust.

38

The combination of throbbing between her legs and her heart hammering inside her chest made it impossible for her to think straight. Controlling lust was easy with a stranger. However, it proved much harder with someone you'd dreamed of nearly every day for two years.

All it took was stripping naked to make her dreams a reality.

Will moved closer and his hot breath brushed against her cheek. What she wouldn't give to feel it against her bare stomach, her thighs, her breasts.

Damn it. So much for being professional about this. She could fight her body, or she could satisfy it and move on.

Petra was honest enough with herself to know nothing would get done until she'd sated her traitorous body's yearnings. After all, one quick fuck wouldn't hurt anyone. Millie should be watching them and would create some sort of distraction if danger approached.

After nodding to his question, Will released her and gave her thirty seconds. Taking a deep breath, she clicked on the scrambler device in one of her many hidden pockets to block out both Millie and anyone listening in. Then she turned to keep an eye on Will in case he tried something.

Yet as she took off her purse, tugged her blue sweater over her head and tossed it to the side, all Will did was drink her in slowly with his eyes. The heat she saw evaporated the last of her reservations; they both wanted this.

Unzipping her pants, she then kicked her shoes off and wiggled out of her pants, careful not to let anything hidden in the pockets fall to the ground; she might need the tools later.

Finally standing in her bra and underwear, she motioned toward Will. "Your turn."

He crossed his arms over his chest. "Not until you're naked."

Damn, the steel in his voice was new. Leyna would've hated it, but Petra liked it far more than she would admit.

Taking one bra strap off and then another, she tugged it down to reveal her breasts. Will growled and her nipples turned to points in response.

She unclasped it. The scrap of material fell to the floor and she placed her thumbs under the waistband of her underwear. Petra could turn back and say no. Hell, she could take out the stun gun from her purse and incapacitate Will before he reacted. But the memory of her finger brushing against his hard cock was the last bit of convincing she needed to tug off her last piece of clothing and raise her hands at her side. "I'm done. Why do you still have your clothes on?"

Will's gaze rose from her body and met hers. She shivered at the hunger she saw there.

He ripped off his shirt and pants. Petra barely had time to drink in the sight of his chiseled abs and long cock jutting from his body before he tore open a condom and rolled it down his dick.

Before she could think about how he'd come prepared and must have expected this, Will had her in his arms. His hands roamed down her back to her ass and he lifted. Out of instinct, she wrapped her legs around his waist, which put his dick against her clit.

Will squeezed her ass cheeks before murmuring, "I hope you're ready because I'm not going to hold back."

Since the scrambler blocked out Millie from hearing their conversation, Petra spoke the truth. "Stop talking and show me."

Descending on her lips, he thrust his tongue into her mouth and pulled her tighter against his hard body. The light hair on his chest tickled her nipples and she dug her nails into his back. Will growled and laid her back on the bed. The full weight of his body only made her wetter.

Will broke the kiss to cup her breast. He tugged her nipple a few times before taking it into his mouth and sucking hard. Out of desire, she pressed his head down, signaling she wanted more. He drew her even deeper between his lips. Despite their time apart, Will remembered her sensitive nipples. She opened her legs even wider in invitation.

She'd missed him.

As Will continued to suck, lick, and swirl her tight bud, her core pulsed. For once, she didn't want extended foreplay. She was more than ready for his cock.

Petra dug her nails deeper into his scalp and he bit her nipple. Pleasure and heat coursed through her body and she moaned. Her other breast was heavy and sensitive, wanting equal attention. Maybe a little more foreplay wouldn't be so bad.

Not that she could think long on that. As if reading her mind, Will moved to tease her other nipple at the same time his fingers found her swollen folds. She cried out as he lightly brushed her sensitive skin.

Will's eyes met hers just before he plunged a finger into her core.

"Will."

His name sounded like begging to her own ears.

As his finger found her g-spot, his thumb brushed against her clit. She was so sensitive she nearly jumped. "Again."

Will growled. "Say my name again."

Lost to her hormones, Petra didn't fight him. "Will."

"Good."

He increased the pressure on her clit as he moved his finger inside her. She already felt the pressure building. Just a few more strokes and she'd come.

41

But then his hand was gone. Opening her eyes, she cried out, "What the hell? Why did you stop?"

~~~

Will's intent had been to fuck Leyna quickly, fulfill his lust, and talk.

However, as soon as he'd covered her short frame with his, her small breasts had pressed against his chest and all but begged for him to suck them.

Even now, with Leyna frowning up at him, all he wanted to do was lick between her thighs until she screamed.

What the hell was wrong with him? The woman had lied and broken his heart. So why did he still ache for her?

Will buried the reason deep inside his mind.

He finally answered Leyna. "I want to feel you as you come." He quickly flipped her over, pulled her hips up until she was on her knees, and pinned her wrists over her head. "Tell me exactly what you want." He lightly brushed the tip of his cock against her clit. "Just this?"

Leyna turned her head. "No. I want what you promised." She widened her stance. "No making love." She arched her hips. "Fuck me."

Bloody hell. Gone was the shy and hesitant woman he'd known. And bastard he was, he liked it. "That's what I wanted to hear."

In the next second, Will lifted her hips and thrust into her pussy. But instead of moving, he remained still. "Damn, you're tight."

Leyna remained quiet a second before murmuring, "I haven't been with anyone since you."

He frowned and burned to ask her why. But then he noticed a jagged scar running down her shoulder and it reminded him of the two years between them. They had established separate lives. This was his good-bye to Leyna and he needed to remember that.

Taking a firmer grip on her hips, Will moved. Slowly at first, but he increased his pace with each thrust. He'd been with a few women over the years, hoping to forget Leyna, but none had ever felt so bloody right. The way she gripped his cock as he moved was the perfect amount of pressure. If he wasn't careful, he'd come before her.

And despite what she'd done, Leyna deserved an orgasm.

Lifting her hips a fraction more, he kept her up with one arm and used the other to find her clit. As he rubbed her bundle of nerves, Leyna moved her hips in time with his thrusts. Will tried to hold in a groan, but when she circled, he failed. "Leyna."

Since pressure built at the base of his spine, Will pressed harder against her tight bud. Judging by Leyna drawing in a breath, she still liked a rough, firm touch on her clit.

The sound of flesh slapping against flesh filled the room and Will closed his eyes. Focusing just on the feeling of being inside Leyna, he stroked her tight bud and it almost made him feel as if they were back in their flat two years ago, when they'd been in love and on the cusp of getting married.

Leyna cried out, "Will. Just a little more."

His own orgasm was close, but he gritted his teeth. No matter what Leyna may have done to him, he wouldn't say good-bye as a selfish bastard.

He gently pinched her clit and Leyna screamed. As she clutched and released his cock, Will gripped her hips with both hands and thrust even harder. Between her tight pussy, the scent of her arousal, and the feel of her warm skin under his hands, Will

43

let go. As his orgasm hit, he stilled and resisted shouting Leyna's name. Because if he did, it would be a sort of claim on her. And the last thing Will wanted was to trust the woman with his heart again, no matter how much his body yearned to fuck her every day for the rest of his life.

CHAPTER FOUR

Breathing heavily, Petra clutched the sheets under her hands and simply reveled in her post-orgasmic haze. Between the pleasure and Will's hard dick still inside her, she could almost forget about her dangerous life avoiding drug lords and completing assignments for money.

Almost.

Pushing aside her past, Petra moved away until Will's cock slipped out and she turned to sit on the bed. The distance helped her to focus. Since the night was still quiet outside, it meant that Millie hadn't set off the warning signal yet, but it could happen at any time. Without lust clouding her judgment, Petra could do what needed to be done—warn Will and break his heart.

She finally met his gaze. The hunger and longing there made her heart skip a beat. She might be able to win Will back if she tried.

No. If she loved him, Petra needed to ensure Will's safety. And as long as her brother's asshole boss had claws in either of them, she couldn't afford to care about anyone long-term.

Clearing her throat, Petra adjusted her position on the bed. "Now that's out of the way, we should talk."

Will's eyes turned hard. The change wrenched her heart, but Petra pushed it aside. Will replied, "I suppose we should. Tell me why you're here, Leyna."

"My original intent had been to break you out of the AMT research facility in Hong Kong, give you a new identity, and disappear. But now that you're working with the AMT system, I need to know why."

Will sat on his haunches. "I was doing it before to seek revenge for your death. Now, however, I'm going to continue the work for myself."

Petra clenched her fingers. "But is experimenting on other *Feiru* really the best way to do it?"

"Don't tell me you're one of those DEFEND anti-AMT crusaders."

DEFEND was an organization fighting to destroy the AMT system and free all first-born magic users. "No, of course not. My work is a bit more dangerous and requires far fewer morals."

Will studied her a second before replying, "All of my test subjects are volunteers. If you know about my glowing hands, then you probably already know that strange abilities have been popping up all over the globe. I need to find a way to stop them. Otherwise, the humans will panic and start hunting us down."

Petra had never been on one side or the other of the AMT debate. Staying alive had always taken precedence. However, after hearing Millie describe what had happened to her brother and her other brother's girlfriend, it was becoming harder to remain silent.

Drawing on her recently gained knowledge from Millie, Petra replied, "I've heard rumors about why those strange powers, sometimes called latent abilities, are showing up now. Have you?"

"I don't put much faith in rumors. And in the past, neither did you."

She raised her brows. "Let's just say that rumors can be a useful starting point."

Will waved a hand. "Then spit it out, Leyna. We don't have a lot of time to beat around the bush."

She didn't miss a beat. "But you had enough time to get laid, apparently."

Will grunted. "It's done and over with. Just get on with it."

Jerk. His brusque tone only helped strengthen her resolve for later. "Fine. The old legends say the appearance of latent abilities signals an upcoming curse; one that can only be stopped by the Four Talents."

"What the bloody hell are you talking about? I've never heard of any Talents."

Petra continued. "Considering all books referring to them were burned in the 1950s, it doesn't surprise me."

"Then how do you know about it?"

She shrugged a shoulder. "I have my ways."

"Well, then go on and tell me these rumors. We don't have all bloody evening."

Petra clenched the fingers of one hand. She was sorely tempted to reach out, grab Will's cock, and twist until he yelped in pain.

She decided that would just waste more time and answered him. "The Four Talents have the ability to manipulate the elements without putting their hands to a certain direction."

Will leaned forward. "That sounds like E-1655's abilities."

"Who?"

Will paused but finally answered, "An elemental earth user who can draw on her abilities without pointing her hands to the north. But no one ever referred to her as a Talent."

"I highly doubt they would considering they reduced the woman to a serial number," she drawled.

Will waved a hand in dismissal. "That isn't important right now. What I want to know is how you found out this classified information."

"My partner for this assignment has connections."

"The would-be attacker from this morning?" Petra nodded. "Do you trust her?"

Petra paused a second before answering. "I think I'm getting there. She easily could've snuck away and left me tied up, or worse. Yet she stuck around to help me."

It was true. Despite Petra's threat of turning in Millie Ward, Millie probably could've escaped if she had wanted to.

Will grunted. "Is there anything else she told you?"

Petra nodded. "If you eradicate the latent abilities, the Four Talents will have no one to protect them and they'll be snatched up by power-hungry humans. Then the curse will lay a sickness over the world and most will die."

"A curse?" Will echoed.

"Yes. According to Millie, it's happened before. The Spanish influenza epidemic of 1918 was actually a curse. It was eventually stopped by the Talents from back in the day."

Will put up a hand. "Wait a second. You're saying somewhere between 20 and 50 million people were killed back then because of a curse?" He gave a bitter laugh. "I somehow doubt that could be kept a secret for this long."

Petra narrowed her eyes. "During a time with no TV, very little radio, and when cameras were expensive and time-consuming to use, it's entirely possible. Even if they really were killed by a flu virus and not a curse, do you want to chance it? Millions of people could lose their lives. Do you want that on your conscience?"

He frowned. "And why should I trust you? You could be making all of this up just to get me to halt my research. There are more than a few who want *Feiru* to expose themselves to the world and destroy the AMT prisons system. How do I know they didn't send you to throw me a red herring?"

She straightened her shoulders. "Look, I risked my life to come here and warn you. I first found out about you being locked up back in Hong Kong. I had no idea your new research dealt with latent abilities. I just felt I owed you for what I did by faking my death. If you don't want my help, then I'm starting to think I'll just leave and you can fend for yourself."

Petra moved from the bed and reached for her bra. However, before she could pick it up, Will took hold of her shoulders and maneuvered her upright. Lowering his head, he searched her eyes. She opened her mouth to demand he let her go when his voice filled the room. "Tell me the reason you faked your death and I'll consider listening to you. And it had better be the truth. Despite whatever life you lead now, I know your tells. I should still be able to judge if you're lying."

Will had no idea the lengths of training Petra had endured, but she knew if she lied in this moment, then Will might go quietly back to his research. If he failed to eradicate latent abilities, he might become a prisoner again. And despite the gulf between them, she couldn't stand the thought of Will Evans being locked away for life, or worse.

In a rare move since changing her identity, Petra told the truth. "My brother got into trouble with a low-level drug dealer who only knew my brother by his street name. So, my twin asked for my help. With my chemistry background, my brother knew I would be able to cook meth. If I agreed to do it for two years, the dealer's boss would allow my brother to live. Not really having a choice in the matter, I created a false identity and agreed."

Will's face softened a fraction. "Why didn't you come to me? My father had the influence to help you."

Petra shook her head. "Not this guy. Believe me, the bribes he doled out would've prevented any legal channel from arresting him."

"Then there would've been another way. If you had truly loved me, you would've talked with me."

Petra's heart twisted. "I hurt you to save you, Will. End of story. Now, will you listen to what I have to say?"

Will's face returned to a neutral expression. A small part of her hated that he could close himself off from her.

Her former fiancé finally answered, "I'll listen but it doesn't mean I have to go along with what you say. For the sake of argument, let's pretend these legends hold a grain of truth. What am I supposed to do about it?"

"I have a friend who will take you somewhere safe in exchange for information on what you've seen and done inside the AMT research facilities."

"And what about you, Leyna?"

"I go back to my life as a mercenary and you never see me again."

~~~

Somehow Will managed to keep his emotions under control.

Bloody Leyna and her wanting to protect everyone but herself. That aspect of her personality hadn't changed over the years. "Trust is something to be earned. This friend of yours has yet to prove anything. Hell, I'm not sure I fully trust you."

"Which is as it should be."

Leyna fell silent. It was hard to believe he'd been fucking her only a few minutes ago.

His eyes flickered to Leyna's small breasts and hard nipples, and his dick twitched. If life were simple, they could block out the world and spend the night having meaningless sex. Well, nearly meaningless sex. If Will closed his eyes, he could pretend it was the woman he'd nearly married under him. It was the closest he'd ever come to turning back the clock to a happier time in his life.

Opening his eyes, he met Leyna's gaze again. It was time to stop pining for the past and to focus on the future. "Do you like this new life of yours?"

She blinked. "What?"

Will shrugged a shoulder. "You seem keen to go back to a life of danger and questionable morals. The old Leyna I knew never would've enjoyed it. I think there's a bigger reason behind it."

"The clock is ticking, Will. I need to know if you agree to disappear or not."

As he studied the toned woman with long hair and a hard expression, a shadow of his old feelings flared. He might never trust Leyna with his heart ever again, but her current life would probably end up killing her. "I survived you dying once and I'm not about to do it again."

Leyna frowned. "What the hell are you talking about?"

He crossed his arms over his chest. "If you want me to run away with your friend and share my knowledge, then I want you to stay near me until I feel I can trust these friends of yours."

"Will, I can't—"

"Either that, or I go back to my work. If you truly want to make up for putting me through hell two years ago, then this is what I want."

Leyna remained silent for about ten seconds before saying, "Fine. But I'm only going to warn you once—if you stay near me, you might become a target. My brother is still wanted by the drug lord I mentioned earlier, who is even more influential and powerful than two years ago. My brother and I managed to get away from his claws, but not on good terms. There's a bounty on our heads and any person looking to cash out on it won't blink twice at killing an extra person or two who stands in the way. I just want to make that very clear."

He studied her a second before replying, "What I don't get is you seem capable of reaching out to friends to try and save me. Why can't you do the same for this drug lord problem?"

"It's not that simple."

"You know what, I'm tired of your secrets. Start making sense or I put on my clothes and return to the AMT facility."

Leyna growled. "He has powerful friends, okay? I have yet to meet anyone with resources who is also clever enough to outsmart him, let alone have the desire to help a lowly for-hire hand like myself."

Will wondered who this mysterious arsehole might be. Not that it was his concern. Leyna had made her choice years ago. "Maybe someday you'll be brave enough to try."

In the next instant, Leyna had Will pinned to the bed with an arm across his throat. "Listen, William. I didn't ask for you to try to fix my life. My only concern is getting your ass out of here and to somewhere safe. I'm not going to ask again, so what's your answer? Are you staying or going?"

It was difficult to concentrate with Leyna straddling his chest. The warmth of her skin and her womanly scent made him want to flip her over and fuck her all over again.

Then she pressed firmer against his throat, making it difficult to breathe. He snapped out of it. His reply was strained as he said, "If you accompany me, then I'll go."

Leyna leaned down and her hot breath tickled his cheek. "Good. I'm going to let you up and you're going to get dressed. After that, we need to lose your tail and flee."

He nodded and Leyna released his throat. After a quick cough, he met her gaze again. "I'm assuming you have a plan?"

Leyna scurried from the bed to where her clothes lay on the floor. "Of course I do." She fished something out of a small pocket in her pants and clicked it. Then she spoke again. "Give the diversion in five minutes. Plan A is a go."

Will heard his mobile phone chirp with some kind of message. Reaching for his trousers, he took out his phone and touched the screen. There was a text and a voicemail.

He quickly opened the text message from Gio and read it: *Break-in. Subjects stolen. Meet at designated location. No contact.*

"Fuck," he muttered.

Leyna walked toward him. "What happened?"

He put up a hand and dialed his voicemail. He and Gio had earlier agreed to use both a text message and a voicemail to confirm identity if something went wrong. After the standard voicemail welcome, it was Gio's voice that came on the line. "There's been a break-in and it's chaos inside. I'll tell you more when I see you. More information to follow."

The message ended and he met Leyna's gaze. "Just how good are you at sneaking out of tight security?"

She frowned. "Why? What aren't you telling me?"

Considering Will had agreed to flee, he may as well tell Leyna the truth. "Someone most likely created a diversion, broke into the AMT research facility, and stole my test subjects."

"The ones with latent abilities?"

"Yes."

"Shit." Leyna turned back to her clothes, tossed the rest on and laid her purse strap across her body. She spoke to whoever was listening in. "Did you hear that?" A pause before Leyna added, "Let's go with Plan C." Another pause and Leyna's growled. "I don't care if I'll owe you another favor. Just do it." With a sigh, she turned toward Will. "If we have any chance at escaping, we need to leave now. Follow my lead and don't speak unless I signal it's okay."

Will tugged on his trousers and slipped on his shoes. "I'll follow, but if someone attacks, I'm not going to run."

Leyna scowled at him. "I don't have time to watch your ass and fight on my own."

He rushed Leyna. She stepped out of the way, but he swung out his leg and swept her foot. As she hopped back to regain her balance, he growled, "Stop trying to protect me. If I need your help, I'll ask for it. I probably have more hand-to-hand combat training than you could even dream of. I wasn't about to allow anyone to perceive me as a weakness a second time."

"A second time?" she echoed.

He pushed the memory to the back of his mind and kept his face neutral. "Isn't the clock ticking?"

She shook her head. "Right. Then stand by and wait for the signal."

He opened his mouth to ask what signal when something exploded next door and the room shook. "What the hell was that?"

Leyna smiled. "Not scared of a little bomb, are you?"

Before he could answer, Leyna rushed to the door and opened it a few inches. He heard the sound of rushing feet and screaming. Looking over her shoulder, she stated, "Showtime."

Then she squealed like a young girl and dashed down the hall. Cursing, Will picked up his shirt and followed her.

CHAPTER FIVE

As Petra rushed down the hallway and pretended to be afraid of the exploding bomb, she stole a glance over her shoulder. Will was only a few feet behind her.

Satisfied he could keep up, she focused on getting out of the building and past the man watching Will, if he was even still around.

Weaving her way through the throng of half-dressed men and women, Petra kept replaying the scene of Will rushing her and nearly knocking her off-balance. Begrudgingly, she admitted to herself that his actions had turned her on a little. She appreciated skill and Will clearly had some.

Maybe when things calmed down, they could spar with no holds barred.

Stop it, Petra. There was no future for her and Will. She might have to stick around until he agreed to stay with Millie and her people, but after that, she was gone.

Yet Will's words about taking charge and finding a way to rid herself of Sean Reilly kept echoing in her head. If she were a trusting person, she might ask Millie if any of her contacts could help.

Too bad Petra trusted people with her life about as far as she could throw them.

Reaching the lobby, Petra swept the room with her eyes for anyone who looked calm or who was heading against the crowds.

That was something a bodyguard would do. But everyone was rushing out of the building, even the staff. If they were lucky, they'd lost the man following Will earlier, on their escape from the restaurant.

Still, she wasn't about to take any chances. Petra moved away from the worst of the rushing crowd and Will maneuvered his way next to her. She whispered, "Follow my lead."

She faintly heard a, "I'm already bloody doing that," from Will's direction, but she was already heading toward the thickest part of the fleeing clientele. Ducking down, she clung to a woman and pretended to sob. The upright woman would shield Petra's face from anyone studying the crush of people fleeing the hotel.

Will came in next to her and stooped down. Instead of sobbing, he kept saying, "Help me, please."

Her former lover played quite the convincing coward.

With no time to think about where he'd picked up that trick over the last two years, Petra kept up her act. Eventually, they were outside and she heard Millie's whisper in her ear. "At the end of the street, turn left. I'll wait behind the second set of bin bags on the left side."

Not wanting to break her cover, Petra kept up her cries and continued to cling to the woman. When they finally reached the end of the street, she took Will's hand and tugged him away from the crowd. While a few people were heading down this street, it was emptier than the main thoroughfare.

Since she and Millie had been headquartering their operations in this part of town, the dirty, dilapidated buildings didn't faze her. After all, she and Millie had already challenged and defeated the small-time gang in the neighborhood. No one would mess with her unless they were much bigger fish, such as an AMT enforcer squad.

Of course, there was little tying Petra to the Sichuan AMT research facility. She doubted the enforcers would waste their time on her. Will, on the other hand, was a different story. At the earliest opportunity, she needed to perform a sweep for tracking devices. For all she knew, someone had slipped one into a pocket or hid it in his shoe.

They approached the second set of garbage bags and Petra tugged Will down to squat next to Millie. Petra didn't waste any time and asked, "Did you see anyone follow us?"

Millie shook her head. "No. Beyond the few scared individuals racing down this street, I haven't seen anyone else. To be honest, I haven't seen the big, bulky man who followed you and Will after leaving the restaurant since you two entered that dodgy hotel."

Petra nodded. "Good. Then we need to focus on getting Will out of here."

Will spoke up. "Not so fast."

She turned her head toward him. "Now is not the time to have regrets or back out. You're coming with us and we need to leave as soon as possible."

Will raised his brows. "If we do, you'll lose a valuable resource."

Petra growled out, "What the hell are you talking about?"

Will nodded to each of them. "You and this woman promise me a favor each later, and I'll tell you."

Grabbing Will's shirt, Petra leaned in close. "I'm not going to negotiate with you or waste any more time talking. We need to haul ass."

Millie spoke up. "What's the resource?"

Petra opened her mouth, but Will covered it with his hand and answered, "Does the name Giovanni Sinclair ring a bell?"

Millie's eyes flashed with interest. "What about him?"

Petra bit his hand, but Will's skin glowed a warm, faint green and he ignored her. "I'm supposed to meet him at a secret location. Agree to my favors and I'll take you to him."

Petra growled at the same time as Millie bobbed her head. "Done."

He met Petra's gaze again. "Well?"

She was tempted to bite him hard enough to draw blood. But since he'd probably just heal himself, it was a waste of energy.

Besides, as much as she wanted to leave the town, Giovanni Sinclair would be quite the catch from a professional point of view. The blackmail possibilities were endless.

Recognizing Sinclair's worth, Petra nodded.

Will released her mouth. "Right, then we need to head to the west side of town."

"That's on the other fucking side. Giovanni might be valuable, but he's worth nothing if we're all dead. The area is probably already crawling with AMT enforcers," Petra bit out.

Millie smiled. "Leave that to me. Gio is worth the risk."

Will frowned and looked to Petra. "What is she talking about?"

Petra sighed in disgust before answering, "Gio kidnapped her, interrogated her, faked her death, and held her hostage. She can't stop talking about him."

Millie stuck out her tongue. "I don't talk about him all of the time."

Petra rolled her eyes. "We don't have time to argue the point."

Millie drawled, "Only because you'll lose."

Will placed a hand on each of the women's shoulders. "So, do we have a deal?"

Millie answered, "Yes. My boss will owe me big time and I can't wait to collect. Now, come on."

Petra jumped in. "Not just yet. Help me check Will for tracking devices."

Millie grinned. "You're inviting me to touch all of those lovely muscles?"

Petra resisted the urge to knock Millie flat on her ass. "Just hurry up and help me."

Millie's hands moved to Will's shoulders and Petra quickly crouched down to feel his leg. Slowly running her hands up, she stopped at his pockets, which put her eye level with his crotch. Resisting the urge to look up to Will's eyes, she inserted her hands into each of his pockets and felt around for anything unusual.

His body heat seared through the material and into her palms. Memories of earlier, when they'd been naked in the hotel room, flashed into her mind.

Petra clenched her teeth. Being near the man was dangerous.

Finishing the lower half check, she ordered, "Lift your shoes."

After checking them, Petra stood. Millie was doing her last checks of his back and arms, squeezing and lingering longer than necessary. However, before Petra barked for the woman to finish, Millie put out her hands and said, "Ta-daa! He's tracker free. Can we go now?"

Millie didn't wait for an answer as she headed down one of the streets. Petra cursed and took Will's hand. She tried to ignore how his large, warm hand engulfed hers. "Let's go before she kills herself."

Will's voice filled her ear. "For someone who claims to not have any friends or people to help, your female partner acts like a friend to me."

Glad to be in front of Will so he couldn't see her face, Petra studied Millie's form. The last few weeks had been both annoying

59

and more fun than she'd ever admit out loud. Not that she trusted Millie completely. The woman had secrets, she was sure of it. "Millie owed me a favor. It's as simple as that."

Will squeezed her hand and she chanced a glance over her shoulder. Yet all she was greeted with was a neutral expression. Will raised his brows. "What?"

Shaking her head, Petra answered, "Nothing."

As they wound their way down one alley and then another, Petra decided she must've imagined Will's reassuring squeeze, unless he was deliberately messing with her head.

Regardless, Petra pushed all of her questions to the back of her mind. She needed to focus on making it out of Sichuan Province alive. And not only that, but also with a prisoner in tow. Giovanni Sinclair wouldn't go down easily. His father, James Sinclair, was a power-hungry, wannabe politician who controlled the *Feiru* High Council and the AMT Oversight Committee with one hand tied behind his back. It was going to take all of her and Millie's experience combined to pull this operation off.

She only hoped Millie's boss would reward them in the end. Petra didn't do charitable deeds. The instant she did that, her reputation as a mercenary would be ruined and people would consider her easy pickings.

Until Sean Reilly was out of the picture and her brother was safe, that wasn't an option.

Picking up her speed, she kept her eyes and ears open as they followed Millie through the streets.

~~~

Millie Ward's heart thumped double-time. Partly because she was nervous, but also because she was curious to see Giovanni again.

True, the bastard had kept her under watch at a remote cottage in Norway for a while. But since the man had had the chance to kill her instead of protecting her, Millie's curiosity burned to know why he'd faked her death instead. Gio's father was one powerful bastard and Millie wouldn't put it past the arsehole to kill off his own adopted son if he found Gio had disobeyed him.

Focus on the prize, Ward, and worry about finding answers later. If Millie didn't make it to the west side of town, she'd lose her chance to see the reserved and powerful man. Not that she wanted to see his brown eyes flecked with gold again or his broad shoulders. Or, to find a way to break his control and see the man hidden beneath the mask.

No matter how much she wanted to find out more about Giovanni, her curiosity was secondary to her ultimate goal of handing Gio over to Millie's boss and resident crazy lady, Neena Chatterjee.

For once, Millie wished the DEFEND co-founder would show up wearing a cape and offer one of her bags of trail mix. Neena was eccentric, but bloody good at getting people out of scrapes. Very few knew of Neena's powers, but Millie was one of them—Neena's foresight ability was helping DEFEND win the battle against the AMT Oversight Committee.

Even so, success wasn't guaranteed. Millie would just have to try her damnedest to escape unscathed. After all, the AMT would only be destroyed if individuals took initiative beyond Neena's predictions. The future was uncertain, but Millie was determined to rid the world of the AMT prisons. Just remembering her brother's screams at being touched sent a rush of anger through her body. They'd put him through a series of psychological tests, which was just a fancy way to say they'd scared the crap out of him in the name of research.

Garrett wasn't the only one suffering, though. The AMT system was little more than an excuse to experiment on innocents. Many more inmates remained trapped inside and needed rescuing.

Her resolve to succeed strengthened, and Millie stopped in front of a low wall to wait for Petra and Will to catch up. She noted Petra holding Will's hand, but didn't comment. The teasing would come later. When they were close enough, she said, "This is the fastest way. However, there may or may not be a slight drop on the other side."

Petra raised an eyebrow. "Then climb up and find out."

Millie raised her brows. "Hey, you're not the boss of me. If anything, you should climb up."

Will tugged his hand free of Petra and stood between them. "I'll do it."

Before either she or Petra could reply, Will reached the top of the wall and pulled himself up with ease. Damn, the man was strong and sexy. If only Petra wasn't clearly still in love with the bloke, then Millie would probably try to lure him into bed. Her dry spell was approaching the year-mark and she wanted some release not brought on by her own hand.

Will lowered himself back down and turned toward them. Millie snapped back to the present when he spoke up again. "There's a ledge about twelve inches wide from the wall. However, there is a thousand or more foot drop beyond that. Provided we're careful, twelve inches is enough space to land without trouble."

Millie snorted. "Says the man who probably has a price on his head by now. If they start firing guns at us, twelve inches won't be enough if we need to jump without taking our time."

Petra pushed Millie aside. "Ignore her. She just likes to whine. We can do it, no problem."

Petra reached for the top of the wall, but before she could jump, Will had his hands on her waist and lifted. Maybe later Millie could lock the pair up in a room and let them hash out their issues. Despite all of Petra's badgering, Millie was starting to like the mercenary. If she played her cards right, she could get Petra and Will to join DEFEND.

Yes, that would be brilliant. The look on Millie's older brother Jaxton's face at netting a healer and a former mercenary would be worth all of the hassle.

Petra scaled over the wall and released her hands. The soft landing didn't result in screaming, so Petra had to be safe. Millie approached the wall and jumped before Will could reach her. Sitting atop the stone structure, she looked down at Petra, noted the woman wasn't in any danger, and then scanned the surroundings. The mountains dropped several thousand feet to a basin below. Falling meant death, but at least the sheer drop protected them from an attack on this side of the wall.

Well, provided the AMT enforcers didn't have a helicopter.

Millie scaled down and landed with a soft thud. She pointed to her right. "This way."

Petra muttered, "Sometimes, I wonder if you chose the hardest path on purpose."

Millie shrugged. "As long as we're quiet and don't fall down the side of the mountain, we should be able to circle the city and reach the west side in no time. Maybe even undetected."

Will landed gently behind Petra. "Then can we go already? I'm not a fan of heights to begin with and only the adrenaline in my body is keeping the panic from creeping up."

Waving toward the basin floor, she murmured, "It's only a one or two thousand foot drop. Calm down."

Turning around, she walked at a brisk pace. Petra would ensure Will followed. All Millie wanted to do was catch Giovanni

Sinclair and she wasn't about to give the bastard enough time to flee.

~~~

Will kept his breathing even and steady. As long as he didn't look to his right, to the valley below, he'd be fine.

Or, so he could try to convince himself.

Despite his various attempts to erase his fear of heights over the years, Will had failed. Watching his brother fall out of the tree as a lad had done its damage. The fact Henry had been confined to a wheelchair for the rest of his life hadn't helped, either.

Leyna glanced over her shoulder. "Hydrogen, helium, lithium."

Her words brought him out of the memory of his brother's fall and back to the present. The corner of his mouth ticked up. "You remember our distraction game."

"Hydrogen, helium, lithium," Leyna repeated.

Aware she would keep repeating the first three elements from the periodic table until he named the next three, he stated, "Beryllium, boron, carbon."

Leyna continued, "Nitrogen, oxygen, fluorine."

As Will and Leyna continued taking turns naming the elements, he forgot about where they were and what was happening. The last time they'd played this little game, it had been from the top of the London Eye Ferris wheel. Leyna had finally convinced him to ride the blasted contraption, but there'd been a mechanical issue when they'd hit the top of the wheel. Reciting the periodic table a few times had helped pass the thirty minutes they'd been stuck there.

He wondered if the game signaled Leyna still cared for him.

He blinked. What the hell was he thinking? It didn't matter if Leyna still cared for him or thought of his well-being. He would find a way to help her escape the drug lord arsehole, but that was it. After running away from Gio and the AMT research facility, Will would be a wanted man. The last thing he wanted to do was involve Leyna in all of it.

True, she could probably handle herself. But there was more to it. Knowing her reasons for abandoning him assuaged the rational half of his mind, but his heart would never forget. Being near her was a painful reminder of what he'd once had and could never have again.

Just as Leyna recited the final element, Millie put up a hand to stop them. After making a "stay put" signal, Millie grabbed the top of the wall and slowly pulled herself up. While she was too young and daring for his tastes, he had to admit he was impressed with the small woman's strength. Unable to restrain himself, he leaned toward Leyna and whispered, "Between you and Millie, I almost want to believe there's an entire army of super women fighting the evils of the world."

Leyna rolled her eyes. "Women can be strong without being superheroes. Most of us do it out of necessity."

He burned to ask another question, but Millie slowly lowered herself down and came as close as she could to them on the small ledge. "This is where we need to climb back over the wall to head west. Where exactly are we going? I need specifics."

Will met the woman's eyes and debated doling out information as they went. However, that would only waste time. Still, he had one last question. "Tell me how you plan to capture Giovanni and I'll tell you."

Millie smiled slowly. "I'll be the distraction and Petra can kick his arse. He'll never see it coming."

"Petra?"

Leyna answered, "That's my name these days."

Will frowned. "Not sure I like it. But regardless, Gio is probably armed and able to take care of himself."

Millie waved a hand in dismissal. "Probably not. He was a university lad before working for his father. He has very little self-defense training, which should make him an easy target."

Will shook his head. "You're wrong. I know he carried some kind of stun gun with him. He probably has it now."

Millie shrugged. "Believe me, when he sees me, he'll be too shocked to whip out the stun gun in time. Petra will have him on the ground with her knee in his back by then."

"What about his bodyguards?" Will asked.

Leyna spoke up. "Do you think he could lose them, if it came to it?"

Will scanned his memory and nodded. "Probably. He's lost a few tails before, mostly in university. With a disguise, it could be done."

Leyna bobbed her head. "Right, then tell us exactly where we need to go and leave the rest to us."

Will scanned Leyna's eyes, which were full of confidence. He had no reason to trust her, but he believed his former fiancée could handle the situation. He went with his intuition. "It's just inside the tree line near the biggest house on the western side of the town. Once there, I'll guide you. I had to memorize the route."

Millie scrutinized him. "Do you think that's wise? Someone could be lying in wait to attack."

Leyna lightly poked Millie. "Leave him alone. He nearly took you out earlier today. Will can handle himself."

For some strange reason, he stood taller at Leyna's words.

Millie rolled her eyes. "In the future, I think we need a rule—no boyfriends allowed on a mission."

Leyna and Will responded at the same time, "We're not—"

Millie cut them off. "Save it. I'm not going to waste time arguing. Get yourself over the wall and follow me." She turned toward the wall but then looked back at Will and Leyna. "And don't waste time snogging, either. Tick, tock goes the clock."

An image of earlier, of when he'd had Leyna naked and in front of him, flashed into his mind. Clearing his throat, he was about to dismiss Millie's claims but the bloody woman had already scaled the wall.

Not giving Leyna a chance to refuse, he took her by the waist and lifted her up. Unlike before, he took advantage of the view and admired the toned muscles of her arse. Back in the hotel, he hadn't the time to memorize the new planes and valleys of her body. And for some reason, he was curious to do so.

All too soon, Leyna was over the wall and out of sight. Her absence helped to regain his wits and focus on the end goal of getting to Giovanni.

It wasn't as if he and Leyna had a future anyway.

Will followed the two women and pulled himself up.

He quickly jumped to the other side. The second his feet touched the ground, Millie and Leyna hurried off in the direction of the large, two-story house in the distance, and he followed.

The silence and lack of Leyna's hand in his gave him time to think. He might've agreed to go with Millie and tell all, but he didn't know Millie's boss or what her people would do with the information. A back-up plan was in order, just in case the woman's boss turned out to be no better than a crazy drug lord or power-hungry politician like James Sinclair.

No matter what others might think, Will had some morals left.

Then there was the problem of Leyna. If he stayed around the woman too much longer, he might start doing something daft, such as forgiving her for breaking his heart and possibly giving her a second chance.

Which he didn't want.

Mostly.

What the hell? Frowning, Will picked up his pace.

CHAPTER SIX

Millie increased her pace as they drew nearer the large, two-story house at the western end of town. She shouldn't care so much about seeing Giovanni again, but not only had her pride been stung, the man was a walking contradiction. Kiarra Melini—her brother's girlfriend and Gio's first-born sister—kept telling stories over the phone of the young lad who'd taken in stray animals and nursed them back to health. How Gio had morphed from that boy to the lackey of James Sinclair was beyond her.

Sure, nabbing Gio would win Millie bonus points with her boss, her brother, and Kiarra, but she would keep him tied up until he answered her questions. Otherwise, she might go mad from the 'what if' questions floating inside her mind.

Reaching the perimeter of the giant house belonging to the town's mayor—bribed heavily by the AMT research facility to look the other way—Millie put up a hand and Petra and Will stopped just behind her. Scanning the area and listening intently, she didn't see or hear anything out of the ordinary. No doubt, the mayor had security inside the compound. However, earlier research had shown there weren't any security cameras due to the AMT Oversight Committee's mandate, which worked to their advantage.

It was still a daft place to have a secret meeting since getting in and out would be difficult for the untrained. And no matter what Will Evans said, Gio wasn't trained for an assignment like this one.

Rather than worry about what could happen, Millie moved to Will's side and whispered into his ear, "Once we're inside the tree line, we should be safe and I'll allow you to lead. For now, I need to know which direction to go."

Will pointed to a spot southwest of the house. With a nod, Millie signaled for Petra to watch their backs before Millie weaved her way toward the spot, careful to stay out of sight.

When they were nearly to the tree line, she heard a small branch break.

One second passed, and then another, but she didn't hear another sound. Maybe it had been a wild animal.

Taking out the stun gun she'd purchased from a contact in China, Millie inched slowly toward the trees. Everything remained quiet until they were all about five feet inside and shielded from view. A large crash sounded from deeper in the forest. Moving through the trees as quickly as she could without giving away her position, Millie readied her gun. When she approached a small clearing deep in the forest, she halted and blinked.

Neena Chatterjee stood over an unconscious Giovanni Sinclair, her foot on his arse and a grin on her face. Neena waved. "Hello, Millie. Right on time."

Millie surveyed the area but didn't sense any other threats. With a sigh, she pocketed the stun gun. "Why didn't you tell me you were coming?"

Neena prodded Gio's arse with her shoe. "Because I need to keep you on your toes." Petra and Will finally emerged from the trees. Neena waved at them. "It's nice to meet you two in person." She growled and made cat claw motions with her hands. "Although you are much more stunning in person, Leyna Grunwald."

Petra aka Leyna frowned and looked at Millie. "Who the hell is that?"

Millie motioned toward the petite, copper-skinned woman with wild, curly black hair. "May I introduce my boss, Neena Chatterjee."

Neena skipped toward them. When she stopped, she took out a baggie and opened it. "Trail mix? I brought my super-secret blend with me today."

Leaving Petra and Will to fend for themselves, Millie approached Giovanni.

Unconscious, the man looked almost peaceful. There was no hardness to his jaw or tension in his forehead. Of course, with his eyes closed, she couldn't see the intelligence or cunning in his gaze. For some odd reason, she wanted to slap his face and wake him up so she could.

But Millie resisted. Her next job was getting Gio out of China. Only then would she have the chance to interrogate the man and get some answers.

~~~

Petra barely had time to refuse the offer of trail mix from the crazy lady before said lady moved between her and Will. Looping an arm around each of their waists, Neena pulled them closer together. For such a petite woman, Neena was strong.

Petra's frown deepened as she looked down at the woman. "You're not what I expected."

Neena winked. "I'll take that as the highest form of flattery." Giving one last squeeze, Neena released them. "But you'll get used to it. After all, you now work for me."

Will spoke up. "Wait a second, who the bloody hell are you, lady? I never agreed to work for anyone."

Neena tapped her chin. "Aw, but you're wrong. You were working for Gio. Then you agreed to give information to Millie's boss, which is moi. Since Gio is now my prisoner, that means you work for me."

Petra took a step toward Neena. "How do you know all of that? I'm pretty sure Millie didn't have time to call you between the bomb, fleeing, and getting here. Who are you, exactly?"

Millie rejoined their group and beat Neena to the reply. "Neena has visions of the future. I don't understand how it works, exactly, but her track record has been 99 percent correct to date."

Neena tsked. "Hey now, that 1 percent isn't my fault. The idiot ate a peanut and died from shock." Neena looked back to Petra. "He did it on purpose, too, the rascal."

Millie rolled her eyes. "Only because you drove him mad first."

Neena waved a hand in dismissal. "It's not my fault if he couldn't understand brilliance."

Petra resisted pinching the bridge of her nose. "How about we forget the statistics and figure a plan to get the hell out of here."

Neena pointed deeper into the forest. "Go that way and a team will help you escape. No enemies should stop you in the next ten minutes. Oh, and this fine man here is free of bugs or anything that can track him. Yet another reason you owe me."

Will spoke up. "I'm not going anywhere until you give me some answers. For all we know, it could be a trap."

Neena looked to Will. "Ah, look who's clever. But I assure you, it's safe. Ignore my help and you won't make it out of here alive." She glanced between Petra and Will. "And I think you two very much want to survive this together."

Petra reached out to grab Neena, but the woman jumped a few steps back. Neena raised her hand. "Ta-ta for now. The next time we meet, Leyna will rise from the dead."

72

Neena turned and skipped into the forest.

Turning toward Millie, Petra shook her head. "There's no way in hell I can work for that woman."

Amusement twinkled in Millie's eyes. "Oh, she's not that bad. And I'd heed her warning. I tried to resist once, and later ended up with a broken leg."

Will muttered, "She probably broke it for you."

Millie looked at him. "Ah, but she doesn't need to do that. Planting a small nugget of an idea in someone's brain will help her years down the line. Neena definitely plays the long game." She motioned toward the forest. "I'm going in the direction she said. You can carry Gio."

Petra growled. "I'm not bloody carrying him alone."

Will moved to the unconscious man. "I'll do it."

She watched as Will squatted and maneuvered Gio's body over his shoulder. Will stood up with ease. Petra was impressed. "You were never that strong in our old life."

She regretted bringing it up, but Will replied before she could dismiss it. "And you had a different name. Do you want to go through everything that's changed or get a move on? I, personally, don't want to loiter around. I like staying alive."

Millie started walking and Will followed. Petra jogged to catch up to him. "I didn't say it to be negative. I'm actually quite impressed with your strength. It means you might not die on our way out of China."

Will adjusted his grip on Giovanni. "I may not like my ability, but I can heal myself. It's going to take a lot to kill me."

Petra raised her brows. "What, such as decapitation? Unless you can regenerate, that would definitely kill you."

Will answered dryly, "I'll try not to get my head chopped off. Does that ease your mind?"

She frowned. "Don't joke about this. When you're on the run, death is always a possibility."

"Says the woman who's been doing it for two years and is afraid to ask someone to help her escape her old life."

Petra was tempted to kick Will in the balls for mentioning her problem in front of Millie.

Millie looked over her shoulder and chimed in. "What is he talking about, Petra?"

"Nothing—"

Will cut her off. "Ask her why she had to change her name from Leyna to Petra."

Millie raised her brows. "Why, Petra?"

"It's none of your concern."

Millie studied her a second before shrugging. "I'll get you to tell me later. Right now, we need to hurry and find this team of Neena's. Being quiet may not hurt, either. And definitely no snogging."

They all fell quiet, but Petra glared at Will for good measure. She was grateful he hadn't spilled her troubles, but hinting was still bad enough. Millie would pester her incessantly.

Petra couldn't wait to be free of everyone and go back to working solo.

Then Will reached out to touch her lower back with his free hand and kept it there. How he managed to keep Gio balanced on one shoulder showed a degree of skill.

She really should move away from him. Will would get the message if she did.

Yet as he lightly rubbed the small of her back, some of her irritation eased. She wondered if his glowing, green light could affect a person's emotions or not because Petra should be pissed off, but a small part of her was glad he'd brought up Sean Reilly and her troubles. After all, Millie and her boss might be able to help her.

If Petra stuck around, that is.

Looking up at Will, Petra burned to know something before she left. Not sure when she'd have the chance again, she blurted out in a whisper, "Earlier, you mentioned not wanting to be seen as a weakness for a second time. What did you mean?"

Will's voice was so low she could barely hear him. "Aren't we supposed to remain quiet?"

"Neena said we should be free of threats for the next ten minutes."

He raised an eyebrow. "And you believe her?"

She touched his side. "Maybe. Consider it a peace offering for you mentioning my past in front of Millie."

He looked at her askance. "I could say no."

"You could."

Will stared a few seconds and sighed. "Fine. A few weeks after your funeral, some blokes came round looking for you. They beat me up pretty badly. One even drew a knife. After that, I vowed I would learn to defend myself for the future." He paused, but Petra remained silent. She was rewarded when he added, "They were looking for you. Knowing what I know now, I think they were tied to your brother's fuck up. It also means you faking your death was in vain."

She frowned. "Not true. While I'm sorry that happened, you would probably be dead right now if I'd stuck around."

He stopped and met her gaze. "And maybe we'd be married with two dogs, living in a quaint house outside of London."

Petra searched her brain, wondering if Will was right. *No.* She'd done the right thing.

She was about to explain how when Millie dashed ahead and peered through the undergrowth. Going on high alert, Petra adjusted her stance and took out the small gun hidden in her purse.

The second Millie snorted, Petra released her hold on the gun. Millie's voice filled the vicinity. "Figures Neena would send you."

A male voice with a British accent answered, "I'm here saving your arse. Have some gratitude."

Millie looked back at Will and Petra. "It's my brother, Jaxton." She whipped her head back around. "And Kiarra? Is she here too?"

An American female voice replied, "Right here. As if I'd allow Jaxton to leave me behind. Neena said you'd have a surprise for us. What is it?"

"Well..." Millie trailed off and motioned for Will to come forward. Just before he reached Millie's position, Millie dashed ahead through the undergrowth. While keeping her eyes and ears open, Petra followed.

As soon as Petra cleared the last of the bushes and other foliage, she saw a helicopter sitting in a clearing, with a tall man who had the same shape of eyes and brow as Millie. Next to him was a short, dark-haired woman. Petra had seen both of them back in a pub in Edinburgh many weeks ago.

Luckily, neither one seemed to recognize her. Petra was about to introduce herself when Will maneuvered Gio to the ground and Kiarra whispered, "Giovanni."

Millie put her hands up. "Surprise. We have your brother."

Petra eyed the woman named Kiarra. All she knew was that Kiarra was an elemental fire first-born and the niece of James Sinclair. Petra had suspected the fire user to be working with DEFEND, the organization fighting to bring down the AMT prison system. The way she was leaning against Jaxton pretty much solidified Petra's assumption. After all, Jaxton Ward was a well-known DEFEND commander in certain circles and DEFEND commanders were rarely allowed to have relationships outside of the organization.

As Petra looked around the clearing, she waited to see how everyone would react. Jaxton was the first one to speak up. "You can have your reunion later, Kiarra. If we don't leave in the next five minutes, we may not make it out of here alive."

Kiarra stared at Giovanni for another beat before she sighed. "I can't believe I'm going to say this, but you're right."

The corner of Jaxton's mouth ticked up. "Pardon? I think I must've misheard you say I was right."

Kiarra opened her palm and a small flame appeared. "Don't rub it in. I have fire and I'm not afraid to use it."

Will spoke up. "How are you doing that? You don't have a hand to the south."

Before anyone could answer, Petra put it together from the legends Millie had told her over the last few weeks. She blurted out, "You're the Fire Talent, aren't you?"

Kiarra closed her hand and the flame extinguished. "Questions will have to wait. Seriously, we need to go. Jaxton, go help—I'm sorry, what's your name?"

Millie answered, "This is Will and Petra."

Kiarra smiled at Millie. "Thanks. Jax, help Will and I'll tell the pilot to ready the chopper."

Petra frowned. "AMT enforcers are bound to be crawling the area after the break-in. I somehow doubt they're just going to allow you to fly out of here."

Kiarra tilted her head. "Oh, we have a few surprises of our own. You'll see."

With that, Kiarra disappeared into the helicopter.

Will still stood at her side, staring at where Kiarra had just disappeared. She couldn't tell if he was thinking about Kiarra's abilities or admiring the woman's petite form. Unwilling to admit she was jealous of the latter, Petra poked his side. "Go help Jaxton. The sooner we're in the air, the sooner you can try to get some answers."

Will studied her a second before replying, "How do you know I want answers? I could be thinking of the upcoming helicopter ride."

"Because if there's one thing that trumps your fear of heights, it's thinking about how to prove a theory. If Kiarra's the Fire Talent, she could be the key to your research."

Will grunted. "Maybe. Maybe not."

She motioned toward Jaxton. "Just go help him."

Petra half-expected Will to argue some more, but he merely walked over to Jaxton.

Will took Gio's arms and Jaxton grabbed his feet. Then the two men slowly maneuvered Gio into the helicopter.

Not wanting to be left behind, Petra followed. She hated entrusting her life to people she'd just met. Petra only hoped she was doing the right thing by following Neena's suggestion and accompanying Kiarra and Jaxton on the helicopter.

Of course, those were her minor worries. Riding in close quarters with Will Evans would truly test her patience and ability to resist him. On her own, she could probably do it. But Millie was bound to meddle.

It didn't help that Petra wanted to know more of Will's past from the last two years. She had a feeling the beating right after her death was just the beginning. She wondered how he had come to work for the AMT, for starters.

Had he bedded many women since then? Told one he loved her?

Clenching the fingers of one hand, Petra growled. *What the hell is wrong with me? It's time to get over him, already.*

Pushing aside her curiosity and anger, Petra boarded the helicopter and took a seat.

CHAPTER SEVEN

Will was careful to pick the middle seat inside the helicopter, putting himself as far as possible from the windows and doors. The ride was going to be pure hell. While he could handle airplanes because of the stable, almost room-like atmosphere, helicopters were loud, jerky, and tiny, with easy views to the land below.

If only Leyna had sat next to him, he might be able to draw off her nonchalant attitude. But she'd been careful to take the seat farthest away from him, across the way and next to one of the doors. He wanted to know why she had done so, but knew it would have to wait. He would find a way to talk to her. After the exchange with Neena, Jaxton, and the others, Will had more questions than answers.

Not to mention it'd been nice telling her about the beating two years ago. It was almost as if that revelation was the first step in bridging the past between them. As much as he wanted to deny it, Will wanted to tell Leyna more.

Yes, more. While he wasn't ready to admit it aloud, he missed his best friend. Maybe, just maybe, if he learned more of her past, he'd be able to find a way to help her. No matter what she'd done before, Leyna deserved a life free of fear and anxiety.

The second Jaxton shut the door, Will snapped out of his head just as the chopper took off. Wanting to distract himself from the small, metal cage he sat in, he asked, "So how are we getting out of here without being shot down?"

Kiarra stared down at a mobile phone. "Three, two, one."

The helicopter jerked for a second before remaining steady. Will chanced a glance out of the side window. Gusts of wind circled around them so strongly he could physically see it happening.

It was almost as if they were inside the eye of a tornado.

Kiarra grinned and looked to Jaxton. "Darius is right on schedule, as usual."

Jaxton grunted and fell silent. Before Will could ask who the bloody hell Darius was, Millie jumped in. "Where are we going now?"

Kiarra answered, "Our eventual goal is the UK, but we have one more pick-up to make in Hong Kong."

Will frowned. "Don't tell me we're visiting the research facility."

Kiarra looked at him askance. "How do you know about that?"

Before he could answer, Leyna beat him to it. "Will used to work there, before his hands started glowing. I'm surprised your strange leader didn't tell you that. She seems to know everything."

He glared at Leyna, but Millie grabbed his left hand and turned it palm upward. "I want to see it. Show us." He tugged his hand, but Millie's grip tightened. "Don't make me have to knock you unconscious."

Jaxton's voice boomed inside the chopper. "Knock it off, Millicent. I need everyone conscious and ready to help retrieve our target. She's irreplaceable."

Leyna waved at Will. "He's also irreplaceable. Will has the power to heal. And if what Millie tells me about the Four Talents is true, he'll be drawn to protecting the closest Talent. Based upon her earlier display of power, I think Kiarra is one."

Will whipped his head around to study the woman named Kiarra. He had momentarily forgotten about his theory surrounding the woman during takeoff. In the present, he eyed the small-boned woman with short hair and delicate features. "How are you a Talent? You look as if you might break in two if I hugged you too tightly."

Leyna snorted. "So now you believe the legends."

He never took his eyes from Kiarra. "Not necessarily. And besides, if she is a Talent, I don't feel a pull to do anything. I call bullshit."

Millie released his hand. "We'll see about that."

In the next second, Millie drew a short knife, slashed the top of her brother's leg, and sat back. "There."

Jaxton barked, "What the fuck was that for?"

Millie winked. "You can thank me later." She moved her gaze to Kiarra. "Jaxton is your Conduit and he's injured. Tell Will to heal him and see what happens."

Will had no idea what the hell a Conduit was, but that didn't matter. He put up a hand. "There's no bloody way I'm going to use the power I despise. As soon as we land, I might just take my chances and go out on my own."

Kiarra studied him a second before ordering, "Heal Jaxton or I can't use my power to the fullest and the eventual disaster will kill us all."

Will's hands started to glow. He cursed and closed his eyes. There was no way he was going to follow the woman's order.

Yet something brushed his cheek and he opened his eyes. Despite the fact no one was touching him, the sensation lingered on his skin and traveled down his neck to his right arm. Moving of its own volition, Will gritted his teeth and tried to hold himself in place. Then Kiarra whispered, "Heal him."

82

FLARE OF PROMISE

Will's hand flared a bright green and energy jumped from his palm to the slice on Jaxton's leg. As the skin knitted together, Will finally gave up fighting and merely watched.

The light danced across the wound, jumping back and forth as if sewing a stitch. When the skin finally pulled together, the light dove into the cut and absorbed into the skin. When the light disappeared, there was no cut or even a scar.

Will never really had the chance to watch the healing process before since he'd always wanted to stop it. But after witnessing it through neutral eyes, he had to admit it was pretty amazing. If there was a way to replicate even a fraction of the process using science, he could help save so many lives.

The only question was—could he ever learn to embrace his powers? His reasons for hating magic were becoming muddier by the second. Leyna was alive and magic was helping him escape China in one piece. Maybe there was a balance to be found.

Still, Will needed more information before he made any decisions. Humans finding out about elemental magic would still cause pandemonium. Yet if the Talents were to stop some disaster, it might be worth it if it saved millions or even possibly billions of lives.

Later on, Leyna was going to help him get answers. Then he could make a concrete decision and sketch out the next phase of his life.

Will's hands dimmed until the light faded completely. He didn't feel more tired than before, which made him wonder how much healing he could do before it would harm him. From what little he'd gleaned from his research, using magic always exacted a toll on the user.

Millie clapped her hands together. "See, I knew it. Whether you like it or not, your power exists to help the Four Talents.

Welcome to DEFEND, Dr. William Evans. We'll keep you busy."

~~~

Petra schooled her face into a neutral expression as the green glow faded from Will's hands. She'd had a theory about latent abilities being connected to Talents, but she'd never had proof.

Until now.

Yet as Millie cheered and mentioned the connection, Will's jaw tightened. Petra knew better than anyone what it was like to be at the mercy of someone without much of a say. No matter how grumpy Will had become, he didn't deserve that life. She needed to protect him.

Petra leaned forward and cleared her throat loudly. Even Millie shut up as all eyes turned toward Petra. "While I like being right, I think there should be some rules governing how a Talent uses a *Feiru* with latent powers. Is there anything about that in those legends of yours?"

Millie answered, "Probably. But don't worry—Kiarra has a huge heart. She'd never abuse her power."

Will grumbled, "Except right now."

Kiarra frowned. "I'm sorry to do that to you, but you're a scientist and can appreciate an experiment. This was something important that we needed to know, although Millie could've handled it better." She crossed her heart. "I promise not to do that again, unless someone is mortally wounded."

Petra pushed. "But what about the other Talents? There are supposedly four of them."

Millie waved a hand. "We have another one on our team and we're en route to the third one. Neena won't let them step out of line."

Jaxton sighed. "Why are you giving away such important information?"

Millie shrugged. "Neena said they were part of DEFEND. Take it up with her."

Will spoke up. "Wait a second, go back. You said we're en route to find another Talent. Are you talking about E-1655, the elemental earth user with abnormal magic?"

Jaxton studied Will and then nodded. "Yes, but how do you know about her?"

Petra watched Will debate something inside his head before finally answering, "I was supposed to study her."

Kiarra and Jaxton glanced at each other. However, before anyone spoke again, Gio groaned on the floor. Millie grabbed his hair and smacked his head on the ground, rendering him unconscious again. She dusted her hands off. "That's only a temporary solution. We're going to need something more long term whilst we're in Hong Kong."

Kiarra glared. "How about not killing my brother, okay? I know he was an ass to you, but let's find out why first."

Millie shrugged. "I know how hard to smack someone's head without killing them. He couldn't be in better hands."

Petra took out a small case from her purse. Opening it, two pre-filled syringes lay inside. "I've got it covered."

Kiarra demanded, "What's in the syringes?"

Petra lifted the first syringe, removed the end stopper, and tapped it as she ensured there wasn't any air in the needle. "One full-strength dose of rowan-berry juice and the second one is a diluted version." She could see the doubt in everyone's eyes, so Petra added, "In a former life, I was weeks away from a PhD in

Chemistry. I know how to drug without killing him. I'll give Gio both doses and he should be out for days."

Millie snapped her fingers. "Give him the full-strength dose first and we'll wake him up. The rowan-berry juice will force him to tell the truth. Once we're done, dose him again and he'll fall unconscious."

Millie was right; rowan-berry juice worked as a truth serum for everyone with even a minute amount of *Feiru* blood.

Even though Petra had just formally met Kiarra and Jaxton, she sensed they were in charge. Looking to Kiarra, she asked, "What do you want to do? He's your brother, so it's your call."

Kiarra's shoulders slumped as she studied the unconscious form of her brother. This probably wasn't the reunion the woman had been hoping for.

Straightening her shoulders again, Kiarra nodded. "Give him the full-strength dose and we'll wake him up." She looked at Jaxton. "Could you question him first? I'm going to need a minute as I simultaneously want to hug and punch him."

Jaxton took Kiarra's hand in his. "Of course, love. I have plenty to ask the bastard—er, your brother."

Watching Kiarra and Jaxton, holding hands and drawing strength from each other, reminded Petra of her past. She looked to Will and met his eyes. Longing mixed with fire flashed in his gaze, but disappeared as quickly as it had come.

Could he be thinking of her as she was thinking of him and how they'd once leaned on one another when things turned difficult? Maybe if Millie and the others could help her with Sean Reilly and free her from his grip, Petra might try rekindling things with Will. It would be nice to have some companionship again. The worst he could say was no.

Millie pinched her thigh, bringing her back from her head. She narrowed her eyes at her pseudo-friend. "Pinch me again,

Ward. If we weren't on the same side, I would dose you unconscious with the rowan-berry juice."

Millie grinned. "But we are. So get to it."

Petra muttered, "I'm not your lackey," as she moved next to Giovanni. Sticking the needle into the muscle of his bicep, she pushed the plunger.

Once the last of the pinkish liquid disappeared, Petra removed the needle and gestured toward the unconscious man. "You seem keen on the man, so I'll give you the honor of waking him up."

Millie answered, "I'm not keen. But I suppose I can do it."

Millie grabbed a water bottle, twisted off the cap, and dumped the contents on Gio's face.

The man woke up sputtering. Once he wiped the liquid from his eyes, he spotted Millie. "You."

He struggled to get up, but his hands and feet were restrained. Millie tilted her head. "You underestimated me, and that was a mistake, Giovanni."

Gio spotted Will next. "Why aren't you tied up, Evans?"

Before Will could answer, Jaxton's voice filled the space. "Because he's on our side, Sinclair."

Gio's head whipped around, but his eyes locked on Kiarra. "Kiarra."

Kiarra sat up a little taller. "Hello, brother."

As the two siblings stared at one another, it suddenly felt as if Petra was intruding on a family matter. Yet there was nowhere to escape, so she merely waited to see how things played out.

~~~

Will almost felt sorry for Giovanni. In their short time together, the man had earned some respect from Will for his intelligence and drive. The only question was whether Gio had managed to use that intelligence in the hectic last minutes of the AMT research facility break-in or not. If he had, then the interrogation under the influence of rowan-berry juice should prove interesting. Gio might have classified information on the research being conducted on the children born inside the AMT system.

It also made him wish he could dose Leyna. He swore she'd looked at him with wanting a few minutes earlier, but he refused to believe it was true. After all, the woman was a professional mercenary. To stay alive in that business meant mastering disguise and schooling your emotions. For all he knew, Leyna was playing an elaborate ruse. To what end, he had no idea. But she had yet to regain his trust.

Jaxton spoke up again and Will focused on the interrogation under way; his own would have to wait. "Tell us why you're in China."

Gio struggled to keep his mouth closed, but he couldn't fight the effects of rowan-berry juice for long. "I wanted to know about the experiments being conducted on the children born inside the AMT."

Kiarra frowned. "What are you talking about? Elaborate."

Again Gio resisted, but lost the battle. "I discovered the information in Edinburgh and tricked my father into allowing me to come here. All children born inside the AMT compounds, regardless if they're first-born with magic or not, are kept inside the facility in Sichuan Province. I wanted to see how they were treated."

Kiarra prompted, "And? How were they?"

Disgust flashed in Gio's eyes. "They're locked up and studied with little supervision and no education."

Jaxton grunted. "Strange that seems to upset you when locking away elemental magic users such as your sister is completely fine."

Gio met Jaxton's eyes and didn't so much as flinch at the anger there. "Keeping first-borns away from the world is for everyone's safety. Besides, it's the law. Keeping innocent children prisoner and not providing basic human rights is not only wrong, it's illegal."

Jaxton leaned forward and looked about ready to attack Giovanni. Only Kiarra's hand on his arm stayed him. "Let's not make this about me right now, Jaxton." She turned her gaze to Gio. "Do you know more about the research than you're letting on?"

Gio answered, "Yes."

Kiarra nodded. "Good. Then you're coming back with us. Neena should persuade you to work with us and we can help with the children. I'm sure that will go along with your strange sense of right and wrong."

Gio's face remained calm and collected. "Why should I help you? The worst you can do is kill me and I don't think you're capable of doing that, Kiki."

This wasn't Will's fight, but the less bloodshed and restriction of information, the quicker they could solve the problem. Regardless of his thoughts on the AMT system, he was 100 percent behind freeing the non-first-born children. "Think about it, Gio. If you want someone to help stand up to your father, then these people are probably your best bet. Hell, they have magic and might on their side. If their crazy leader also possesses the abilities Millie claims, then we might be able to work out an end goal all of us can live with."

Jaxton snorted. "I highly doubt it."

Gio studied Will a second before answering, "You have much to gain from an alliance, but I don't."

Millie muttered, "Now who's sounding like their maniacal uncle-slash-adopted-father?"

Anger flashed in Gio's eyes, but vanished in the next second as he answered Millie, "Don't pretend you're so much better than me. We all have our reasons for doing what we're doing."

Millie scoffed. "Perhaps. But I wish to help people whereas you only want to help yourself."

"I think you're doing this to prove something. I don't know what yet, but I'll find out eventually," Gio stated.

Millie buffed her nails against her chest and held them out. "Try your best, posh boy. You'll only fail."

Leyna jumped in. "It's clear we're not going to get anywhere with him during the helicopter ride. I say knock him out and deal with him later."

Kiarra leaned forward. "Just one more question. Do you know that James Sinclair killed our parents?"

Gio frowned. "No, because that's not true. They died in a car crash."

Kiarra shook her head. "You're wrong. He wanted me locked away, and you as his heir. He staged a car accident to kill our parents. There are several sources to prove what I'm saying is true."

Gio's voice was a little less firm as he answered, "I don't believe you. My father is ambitious, but not a murderer."

Kiarra shrugged. "It doesn't matter. You will believe me eventually." Kiarra looked to Leyna. "You can give him the second dose now."

Will jumped in with one more question. "Wait—do you know who kidnapped my test subjects?"

90

Gio met his gaze. "No. But some of the staff were following the orders of some woman. Even though I was in the next room, I still felt compelled to follow her commands. Only once I plugged my ears with my fingers did I rid myself of the feeling and was able to escape."

Kiarra and Jaxton shared another glance. Will looked to the pair. "What aren't you telling us?"

Jaxton shook his head. "Not now. Help us with our mission and I'll tell you more." He moved his gaze to Leyna. "Give him the second dose."

Leyna took out the second syringe, removed the stopper, and cleared the needle of air. "My pleasure."

In one quick motion, she knelt next to Giovanni and injected the diluted rowan-berry juice. The action reminded Will of just how graceful and quick Leyna had become. Not that he wanted to encourage her drugging individuals on a regular basis, but maybe her grace would translate to other areas of her life.

Maybe, if they all survived the ridiculous mission in Hong Kong, he could find out exactly how.

A few seconds later, Giovanni's eyes closed and his body slackened.

Will broke the silence. "So, what's the plan?"

CHAPTER EIGHT

Six hours and another helicopter change later, Petra peered out of her window to watch the landscape as they passed over it.

Unlike Will, she loved heights. Looking at the ground from this height made her feel as if she were a bird. All of the tiny houses and buildings below contained normal people living their normal lives. At one point, she'd scoffed at ever becoming boring. However, after the last two years, she would kill to wake up in a house with two-point-four kids and a dog.

Okay, maybe not the kids just yet. But she could do without constantly looking over her shoulder.

Not that it would happen anytime soon. She had this current mission to finish, Will to deal with, and she still had to figure out a solution about what to do with Sean Reilly.

Since the latter two problems would have to wait, Petra focused on rescuing the elemental earth user.

They would arrive in Hong Kong shortly and land on the private helipad owned by a DEFEND supporter. While the AMT research facility had moved E-1655, she was still in Hong Kong in a unique facility, according to Kiarra and Jaxton.

Keeping the elemental earth user in the city seemed like a stupid idea to Petra. But, hey, the AMT didn't always make the best decisions, despite their public image of running a squeaky clean and efficient operation.

On the other hand, as she surveyed the others inside the flying vehicle, Petra was starting to admire some of DEFEND's tactics and planning. Jaxton Ward's plan was as detailed as she would've done. And while Neena Chatterjee might be a little bit crazy, Petra liked her "I don't give a fuck" attitude. Petra wished more people were as open. The world would have far fewer secrets.

An arm bumped against hers, bringing her out of her head. Petra forced her face into a neutral expression before meeting Will's eyes. He'd muscled his way into sitting next to her at the helicopter transfer.

Staring into his chocolate brown gaze, she ignored the heat radiating off his body as well as his familiar masculine scent. For hours, both had been bringing back memories of her past. Such as the way he'd tease and needle her until Petra got angry. Then he'd put on his brown puppy dog eyes until Petra would sigh with a smile. A few brushes of his fingers, and she'd even jump into his arms.

Will had always pushed her buttons, but he'd also been able to make her melt in the next second. She missed the comfort they'd once shared as well as the trust she'd never experienced with another.

Only with Will had she ever felt safe enough to lie naked with her back to him.

Petra resisted clearing her throat. No matter how much she pretended she didn't want her old life again, there was a longing buried deep within her heart for exactly that.

Will poked her arm. Not willing to acknowledge the sizzle at his touch, she concentrated on his words. "As much as I don't like my newfound ability, I just wanted to let you know that if you get hurt, I'll heal you."

She raised an eyebrow. "Considering the depths of your hatred for magic, that's a pretty big offer."

Will grunted. "I'm being serious, Leyna."

"Call me Petra. Leyna died two years ago."

He hesitated before brushing her cheek. "You'll always be Leyna to me."

The light touch of his fingers sent a jolt of electricity racing through her body. Damn, she'd missed his warm, rough fingers.

She resisted leaning into him. Her voice was strained to her own ears. "Then you're going to be sorely disappointed, Will. Even without danger looming over my head, I can't go back to being that version of myself. I've done and seen too much. Besides, even if it were possible, I would probably get bored."

He stroked her skin some more. "I find it hard to believe your love of science disappeared with the identity change."

"My scientific ability is what landed me in this mess in the first place."

His fingers stilled. "I thought it was because of your brother."

She darted a quick glance toward Kiarra, Jaxton, and Millie sitting in the seats on the opposite side of the bay, but their heads were together planning. Gio had also been handed over to another DEFEND party when they'd changed helicopters. The pilot and co-pilot were focused on flying the helicopter.

Seizing the semi-privacy, Petra murmured, "It was both."

He tilted his head. "Then why can't you be a scientific genius who just also happens to be a badass?"

"Yes, because butt-kicking scientists are handy," she drawled.

The corner of his mouth ticked up. "They can be. Besides, you have field experience most scientists don't. If you decided to put all of your knowledge to good use, you'd become quite the force to be reckoned with."

She raised her brows. "If you're trying to sweet talk your way into my pants, it's not going to happen."

Will leaned closer. His hot breath tickled her ear as he whispered, "No, as I recall, you liked me pinning you against a wall."

The image of Will besting her back in the shady hotel rushed forth. Damn the man and his own strength. "Not true."

He nipped her earlobe. "Liar."

Petra's heart pounded in her chest. She should push Will away and focus solely on the mission.

She searched his eyes, full of curiosity. Maybe this was the time to talk with Will. She'd been putting off this conversation with her former fiancé for far too long. After all, something could go wrong in Hong Kong and she'd lose her chance.

The only question was—how much would she tell him?

~ ~ ~

Will was gambling his chance with Leyna, but he was tired of waiting. Either of them could die in the bloody daft operation to rescue the magic user. He'd lived two years of regrets and what ifs; he wasn't about to risk reliving that again.

Nuzzling her cheek, she sucked in a breath as his short-clipped whiskers brushed against her skin. He'd kept a close-cropped beard all of these years because Leyna had always loved the feel of it. The sight had been a visual reminder of what he'd lost and what he fought for.

He turned his torso further until he was blocking half of her chest from the view of the others. Casually brushing the side of her breast with his forefinger, he whispered, "No matter what you've been through or what name you use, you can't deny the attraction between us."

He waited to see what Leyna would do. He more than expected her to bat away his hand and punch him in the groin.

95

Yet with each stroke of his finger, she leaned a fraction more toward him.

Leyna murmured, "Attraction means trouble."

"Perhaps." He moved his finger a little more until it made contact with her taut nipple. "But can I tell you a secret?"

Holding his breath, Will waited for Leyna's response. How she reacted to his current actions would determine if he had any sort of chance with her or not.

Leyna cleared her throat, but didn't move away. "What? That you've turned into an exhibitionist?"

He let out his breath and chuckled. "What would you say if I had?"

Leyna tilted her head. "Then I'd say there's no way in hell I'm allowing it to happen here. Millie would never let me live it down."

Strumming her nipple, he answered, "While intriguing, it's not what I was going to say."

She sighed. "Will, we're not going to die. The operation is pretty standard and we have the element of surprise. Don't say things just because you want to clean your slate. You might regret it afterward."

He stilled his fingers and met her eyes. "The only regret I have is not telling you every day we were together how much I loved you. And I have another secret."

Her voice cracked as she asked, "What?"

His heart beat double-time, but this might be the only chance he had to speak the truth before he talked himself out of it. "I still do."

She shook her head. "I call bullshit. You clearly hated me when we reunited yesterday. Don't deny it."

He took her chin between his thumb and forefinger, to ensure Leyna couldn't look away. He growled out, "Did you ever think it wasn't because of my hatred of you but rather toward myself? For years, I imagined what it must've been like for you, alone on that fateful night, being burned alive. If only I hadn't put my work above the love of my life and best friend, I might still have her. Seeing you was like seeing a ghost, and at first, I was angry, but mostly because of lost time. The two years between losing you and finding you were the two longest and loneliest years of my life."

Leyna searched his eyes and he wished he had the ability to read minds.

Finally, her eyes turned wet and he'd bet his life it was the first time Leyna had shown even a flicker of true emotions in months if not years. He gently pushed, "Tell me what you're thinking."

He could barely hear her when she answered, "I can't. It will risk your life, Will."

He cupped her cheek. "I can take care of myself. Besides, if I'm injured, I can just heal myself and continue to fight at your side."

She gave a weak smile. "So now you're happy about your magical abilities?"

He laid his forehead against hers. "If it ensures a second chance with you, Leyna, then I will proudly show it to the world if you let me kiss you right now."

"But the others."

He raised his brows. "Now you're going to be shy?" He smiled. "How about you just go along with my exhibitionist desires?"

She snorted. "I'm afraid to do that. It'll bite me in the ass later on."

He moved his hand to the side of her neck. "Woman, I've waited two years for this chance. And I'm tired of waiting."

Before Leyna could reply, he kissed her.

She could've pushed him away, but instead, she parted her lips in invitation. Slipping his tongue inside, he groaned at her taste. He would never get enough of it.

Someone whistled in the background, but he ignored it and took the kiss deeper. Each stroke or flick of his tongue was another claim on his woman.

Despite the mountain of issues still between them, Leyna Grunwald was his once more. No matter what happened, he would be there for her when she needed him and he was never going to let her go again. Life had given him a second chance. Will wasn't about to take it for granted.

~~~

Petra could barely think as Will stroked and licked as he tried to dominate her mouth. She fought back, meeting and tangling with his tongue. While their kiss back in the shady hotel had been good, this one was mind-blowing. Will wasn't just kissing her, he was claiming her.

And she was determined to claim him back. She wanted to keep her sexy warrior scientist and learn everything about him all over again.

Hell, together, they might even achieve her dream of normalcy and safety. Will was the only one who might be able to bridge her old life and new.

Threading her fingers through his hair, she dug in her nails. Will's groan sent a rush through her body that ended between her thighs.

Someone cheered, but Petra didn't care. After so many years of loneliness and surviving on her old memories, she wanted to make new ones. Who knew when a chance like this one would crop up again.

Yet as Will maneuvered her onto his lap, something niggled at the back of her mind about why she needed to stop. Then he grabbed her ass and pressed her against his erection, and she forgot about everything but the hardness of his cock pressing against her.

Everything about William Evans just felt…right. How she'd convinced herself she'd be better off without him, she had no idea.

All Petra knew is that she wanted to give him a chance.

Someone poked her back and yelled, "We're getting close. Save it for later, Petra."

Millie.

With a growl, Petra broke the kiss and glared at the other woman. "Mind your own business, Ward."

Millie placed her hands on her hips. "No. Friends don't let friends have sex in a crowded helicopter. Especially when my brother just happens to be here too." Millie leaned down and whispered loudly, "But I can help you get some later. I have plans and connections. Your own private lovefest will be worth waiting for."

It took a second for Petra to absorb that Millie called her a friend.

Luckily, Will answered so she didn't have to. "How much time do we have?"

Leave it to Will to regain his head and focus on the details. That aspect of his personality hadn't changed.

Millie answered, "Five minutes. Enough time for you to think of grannies and get rid of your hard-on."

Petra narrowed her eyes. "Don't think of his erection."

Will sighed. "Could we not discuss my cock in front of company?"

Millie pretended he hadn't spoken. "Then don't dry hump him. Any straight guy, regardless of the woman on his lap, will react to a little friction."

Will growled out, "She's not just any woman."

Millie shrugged. "Whatever floats your boat. Just get ahold of yourself."

She walked away and Petra looked to Will again. Smoothing his frown, she murmured, "Forget about her. If I'm honest, we should be thanking her."

Will's gaze shot to hers. "Why? Do you have regrets?"

"I mentioned nothing about regrets."

"But do you?" he asked softly.

Petra paused as she stroked the whiskers of his cheek. If there was ever a time to close off her heart and back away, there was no time like the present.

However, the thought of losing Will a second time twisted her heart. Kissing him had released a flood of emotions and memories that she didn't want to wall back up.

Petra wanted a future with Will Evans.

She finally murmured, "No. But I'm concerned about you focusing once we step off this helicopter."

He smiled and lightly slapped her hip. "Keeping me on the helicopter will drive me crazy. The second my feet touch the ground, I'll be ready." She raised her eyebrows. "Just maybe don't bend over in front of me, if you can help it."

Petra snorted. "At least you're honest."

Will gripped the back of her neck. "From here on out, we both need to be honest for this to work. There are still mountains of secrets and two whole years of separate lives between us. We can't afford to add more to the pile."

Her heart skipped a beat at the thought of only telling the truth. Keeping secrets was the reason she was still alive.

Yet as she stared into Will's brown eyes, no deceit lurked there. Only open anticipation and longing.

Nodding, she leaned down to his ear and whispered, "I agree if you agree. But I also have one more promise to extract from you."

She felt the rumbling in his chest as he asked, "What?"

"I want you to stop loathing your gift and keep an open mind."

Placing his fingers on her cheek, he steered her head toward him until he could see her eyes. "I've despised magic for so long that it's going to take some time."

"I can live with that."

He placed a gentle kiss on her lips. "Then I'll try. Any last pointers before we land?"

She frowned. "Don't get yourself killed."

With a snort, he finally released his grip on her and Petra moved back to her seat. She expected Kiarra, Jaxton, and Millie to be studying their nails or looking the other way. Instead, Kiarra and Millie were smiling at them; even one corner of Jaxton's mouth was turned up. Petra narrowed her eyes. "What?"

Jaxton shook his head. "Nothing. Let's go over the plan one more time. Are you two ready?"

Will took her hand in his and nodded. "Ready."

Jaxton leaned forward. "Right, then here's what we're going to do."

As Petra listened to Jaxton's voice, she swore a flare of heat shot up her arm from Will's hand. A quick glance revealed a faint green light emanating from Will and dancing along her arm. The light didn't hurt; it was just a warm tickle.

Since it looked as if she was going to be working with Millie's crazy boss and family, Petra would need to dig into the *Feiru* legends and see what she could find. There was so much unknown about latent abilities and she would do anything to make sure Will didn't accidentally hurt himself or others. Because even though he healed, sometimes magic worked in strange ways. She needed to protect not only herself, but also her man and newish-friend, Millie Ward.

Chapter Nine

Per the plan, Will remained in the middle of their little rescue party as they made slow progress through the trees and undergrowth of the forest. While he had a couple of years of self-defense training under his belt, he'd never actually had to use it in the field like they would be during this rescue. And that made him a slight liability.

One he hoped to rectify in the coming months. Will was damned if he'd let Leyna try to solve the issue of her brother and the drug lord on her own. Especially since they had no idea if Millie or anyone else working with her would help Leyna with that little problem. He might be able to call in his favor from earlier with Millie Ward, but there were no guarantees.

And no matter the cost, Will wanted to make sure Leyna was free to live her life as she wanted. Admitting he still loved her was a huge step, but it was the truth. He could never get back the two years they'd spent apart, but he was going to try his damnedest to make up for lost time.

Well, once they finished the mission.

Jaxton raised his arm and gave the signal to stop. Will listened intently, but he couldn't make out anything special apart from the wind rustling in the trees. They were in the Outlying Islands of Hong Kong and this particular one was the least inhabited. A few of Will's colleagues from the Hong Kong research facility had spent some of their holidays and weekends in the more rural Islands District, but he was pretty sure the island under his feet was privately owned.

It was a strange choice for where to stash away and imprison the magic user. Will would've expected the researchers to keep E-1655 high above the ground to protect themselves. While no one knew exactly how far away from the earth a magic user could still move it, distance was always used as a precaution.

Maybe when he started the next chapter of his life with Neena's group, Will could do some tests to better understand the range of elemental abilities. If he believed the legends and a disaster was coming, knowledge could help the Talents and their army.

Trying not to think about how much his world had changed in the last few days, Will waited for Jaxton's order.

Jaxton finally motioned forward and they continued silently making their way through the forest. The light was growing faint and Will could barely see.

When he bumped into Kiarra's back, he murmured an apology. She pointed up. He followed her finger and his jaw dropped.

High above them was a large rectangular box hanging in place by wires attached to the top and bottom of the container. The wires ran from the edges of the rectangle to the poles stationed every few feet around the structure. Each pole was topped with faint glowing orbs. Scanning what he could in the dim light, his eyes landed on a raised drawbridge-type structure secured between two of the poles with wire.

If that wasn't enough, another platform stood about halfway between the structure and the ground. Judging by the faint light shining through several jagged holes, the elemental earth user had been taken off the drugs long enough to use her abilities there.

Even though Will had previously had high security clearance at the Hong Kong facility, he had never known of the structure's existence. He wondered if it was new. If so, they had built it bloody quickly.

Petra was right behind him, and she tugged his shirt until he retreated. Their party continued back the way they had come for ten minutes before Jaxton spoke up again. "We should be beyond their range for any microphones or sensors here. While Neena had mentioned the structure being unique, she never said it was dangling in the bloody sky. We need to alter our plan."

Will frowned. "To what? If we had an elemental wind user, or even an earth user, it would be easier."

Kiarra answered, "We'll have one once we rescue the woman. For now, I say we draw out whoever is inside the structure. If I create a flame on the underside and warm up the floor, they should evacuate."

Petra jumped in. "And what if they leave her inside? I'm pretty sure your boss doesn't want a barbecued Talent."

Kiarra waved a hand. "I can lessen the heat of the flames with Jaxton's help. More often than not, the illusion is enough to scare away the enemy."

Will had a few words he wanted to say to the cocky woman, but he kept his mouth shut. With all he'd learned lately about magic, it was entirely possible Kiarra could do what she said.

Jaxton pointed at Will. "You'll standby to help, if needed. Even if we all survive without a scratch, we have no idea what shape that magic user will be in."

Only because they'd agreed to keep the secret of E-1655 being a Talent did Jaxton not refer to her by her rightful title.

Will nodded. "I'll try my best, but don't expect for me to perform miracles. Like with any skill, it takes time and practice to refine it."

"I understand that more than anyone," Kiarra murmured.

"Right," Millie chimed in. "Then while Kiarra does her flame trick, I propose Petra and I take care of the fleeing researchers and other staff. If one of them escapes, it might cause a headache for us later on."

Jaxton grunted. "Fine. But I want them alive. I'd like to bring a few of them back to base and question them."

Millie raised her brows. "Of course they'll be alive."

Jaxton muttered, "Just making sure. You get a little enthusiastic sometimes, Millie."

Petra spoke up. "I'll make sure she behaves." Millie opened her mouth, but Petra beat her to the reply. "There's no time to argue. If nothing else, then consider me your operation partner. We'll keep each other in check."

Millie slapped Petra's shoulder. "Good. Glad to see you're finally seeing me as your equal, Brandt."

"Enough," Jaxton jumped in. "The longer we stand here, the greater the chance we'll be discovered. Let's go."

He turned and walked back toward the structure. As everyone followed, Will looked to his hand and imagined a gash that needed healing. It took a second, but his hand flared before returning to normal. He was ready.

Will only hoped his healing ability was unnecessary. Small cuts were one things; he had no idea what to do if someone's life depended on him.

~~~

Petra stood about ten feet behind the two poles holding up the drawbridge structure, hidden behind a few trees and some bushes. Millie was at her side, thankfully remaining silent for a change.

Both of them waited for Kiarra to jumpstart their plan.

The wind rustled through the trees and a bird flew overhead. If the people inside the rectangular container knew of their existence, they were keeping quiet about it.

The only good thing about the weird structure was that it was easy to see who came and went. No one could escape through a hidden tunnel.

An eight-foot-high flame leapt into the air. At the bottom of the blaze, Petra could make out the dark, silhouetted figures of Kiarra and Jaxton. She had no idea why Kiarra leaned against Jaxton or how the flames licking both of their bodies weren't burning them alive. It must be yet another secret related to the Talents.

In the next second, the flame surged until it danced across the bottom of the floating container. Petra half-expected it to catch fire and burn, but while the flames surrounded the box, the exterior paint didn't peel or change in any way as it would in a normal fire.

Still, as the only door to the structure opened and the drawbridge lowered via a remote, the magical fire must still be hot. Various voices yelled for someone named John to hurry up.

While the drawbridge lowered, a metal ladder descended from the drawbridge platform above. Petra looked to Millie and nodded. Millie gave a thumbs-up and the pair of them readied their stun guns.

The bridge clicked into place and people scurried across. Between the green glow from the orbs on the poles and the fire blazing around the rectangular structure, the six people above were as visible as if they'd been standing in broad daylight.

Two of the six remained calm and were ushering the others to safety. Petra would bet her life the two calm men were some type of guard. Turning to Millie, Petra whispered, "Wait until they rush into the forest. I'll take the two guards. You take the other four."

Millie answered, "That's almost fair, although I could do with another two or three."

She glared at Millie. "I'll keep that in mind." Petra waved above. "Once we have this group, I'll go above to find the magic user. You can stay here and watch over the prisoners. Make sure to cover me."

"Of course. I'm not about to allow my new bestie to die so soon."

Petra blinked at being called Millie's bestie, but pushed it aside as people began to descend the metal ladder from the platform. As the first person set foot on the ground, the woman wearing a white lab coat headed straight toward them. Millie and Petra's earlier assessment, that the researchers used the faint trail they were standing in regularly, had been correct.

Just as the escapees were coming into range, one of the guards up above raced back into the structure. Petra whispered, "Damn. Let's take these people down. I need to ensure that guard doesn't kill the magic user."

Millie answered, "They'll be in perfect range in four, three, two, one. Now, come to mama."

Ignoring her, Petra moved a few feet to the side. Trusting Millie to take care of the researchers, Petra followed the slow, calculated movements of the guard currently descending the stairs.

Cries came from her left and the guard jumped the last few feet from the ladder. Just as the guard went to draw his gun, Petra charged at him and fired her stun cartridge. It made contact, but just as it pumped electricity into the male guard's body, he swung his gun barrel against the wires, severing the connection.

Pocketing her weapon, Petra rushed him and landed a kick in his stomach before he could react.

Not that she had time to gloat. In the next instant, the guard regained his composure and moved to the side. Petra took a step to her right and the guard matched it. As they continued circling one another, Petra scanned for weaknesses. Each second she spent with the guard in front of her was another second the magic user's life might be in danger.

However, the guard was in prime physical condition and didn't appear to have any injuries. Petra had a few tricks up her sleeves, but as she noted the silence from behind her, she had an idea. Millie must have her prisoners contained. For the first time in years, Petra was going to count on someone having her back. She only hoped Millie pulled through.

Petra stopped and raised a hand out, with her palm upwards. "Stop right there or I'll use my own magic. Given how you've been protecting the elemental earth user, I'm sure you know what type of destruction I can cause."

The guard cocked his head. "Then prove it."

She raised her voice and hoped Millie would hear her. "I'm warning you. I control lightning and electricity. Come any closer, and you'll feel a jolt like you've never felt before."

Ignoring her, the guard charged. Petra did a back flip and rolled a few feet away. "Millie. Now."

Petra landed on her back as Millie ran out of the forest and discharged her stun guns. The guard barely had time to do more than blink before both cartridges hit their target and zapped the man full of electricity. He dropped like a stone and twitched a few times before going still.

Jumping to her feet, she ran up to where Millie was flipping the guy over. Petra murmured, "Thanks."

Millie winked. "No problem. I love tying up big, buff guys. Now, go. A woman's life depends on us."

With a nod, Petra ran to the ladder and jumped up. She climbed it quickly, as if fire were creeping upward, under her feet. She made it to the drawbridge platform just as the guard came out carrying an unconscious woman wearing a hospital gown.

He met her eyes and moved so that he held the woman over the side. "Step any closer and I'll drop her."

Since the drawbridge was at least thirty feet above the grass, the magic user would most likely die if she fell.

Petra stood her ground. Maybe reason would work with the guard. "There's no way for you to escape. If you go back into the structure, you'll cook. If you jump, you'll probably break your neck. And I'm blocking the exit. But if you surrender, I can at least ensure you'll live."

The guard's gaze flicked behind her and back. "You're wrong."

Petra opened her mouth but the guard charged. She half-expected him to toss the magic user off the bridge. Instead, he tossed her at Petra. She caught the slight woman, but lost her balance.

Unable to regain her footing, Petra made a split-second decision. She used every muscle in her body to toss the woman back onto the bridge. The action caused Petra to push back and fall over the side.

As she fell, Will's face flashed before her eyes. Petra's only regret was not telling Will she still loved him.

The regret didn't last long. Her leg bashed against the smaller platform below and pain shot through her body. She barely had time to scream before the world went black.

CHAPTER TEN

Will crept up toward the battle scene bit by bit until he was only a few feet from the tree line. He barely had time to stare in wonder at the giant column of flame before the figures on the drawbridge above caught his eye.

Leyna stood about eight feet away from a man carrying an unconscious person.

Even knowing Leyna could more than take care of herself, his heart beat double-time. He should be up there, helping her.

And yet, he was stuck hiding in the forest. Clenching his fingers, Will decided he would do whatever it took to be able to fight at Leyna's side in the future. He'd thought he'd failed her two years ago. He never wanted to experience that feeling again.

In the next beat, the man above rushed and tossed his burden at Leyna. While it had to be less than a second, Leyna stumbling and finally tossing the woman onto the bridge played out in slow motion.

Then he watched Leyna fall.

Not caring about his life or Jaxton's bloody plan, he rushed out of the trees. Leyna's leg smacked against the lower platform and she screamed.

He pumped his legs harder.

But no matter how fast he ran, Will would never be able to catch her.

Right before Leyna made contact with the ground, a cyclone of fire appeared under her body. While the force of the spin didn't stop her descent and Leyna crashed to the ground, it might have just slowed her down enough to save her life.

He reached her side. A quick check revealed a bone sticking out of her lower leg. Since fixing her leg would mean nothing if she were dead, Will placed two fingers at her carotid artery. While faint, Leyna still had a pulse.

Quickly checking her head, there was a blow at the back and a lot of blood. It was entirely possible the wound could kill her.

If he didn't do something, his Leyna could die.

Placing his hands on her head, Will closed his eyes. Each beat of her heart was a tap against his skin. He imagined the bone reknitting in her skull, any swelling going down, and all hemorrhaging ceasing.

Over and over he imagined her brain whole, pink, and free of any bruising or bleeding. He was concentrating so deeply that it took him a second to realize Leyna's heart had stopped beating. Opening his eyes, he barely noticed the faint glow around Leyna's body. Moving his hands to her heart, he pressed against her chest to begin CPR. All the while, he switched the image in his head to one of a steadily beating heart.

Leyna's torso jolted with some unseen force and then again. Will moved to breathe air into her lungs when a faint thumping reverberated throughout his body.

Checking her pulse, Leyna's heart beat again.

Will barely had time to acknowledge the relief that coursed through his body. His eyes were heavy, drooping from exhaustion. However, he tried to concentrate again. Even if he burned out from overusing his magic, it would be worth it if Leyna lived.

Just as he started to reimagine his Leyna whole and hearty again, a faint orange blaze mingled with the green light. He looked up at Kiarra's weak voice as she said, "Let me help. Tell me where she's hurt."

His curiosity wanted to know how an elemental fire user could help, but he didn't have time. He'd take whatever he could get. "She hit her head and might have hemorrhaging. While her broken leg looks worse, if we can't ensure she's free of brain trauma, she might not wake up."

Kiarra nodded and the orange glow intensified. She answered, "I'm not at full strength, so we're going to have to work on this together. I'll have to stop if I think I'm going to pass out, though. You need to do the same."

Rather than argue the point, Will nodded. However, if it took his life to save Leyna's, he would give it gladly. "Right, then imagine a brain, pink, healthy, and free of injury in three, two, one, now."

Will kept his eyes open as he focused on healing his Leyna. The green-gold light coursed over and caressed her body. With each second that passed, her heartbeat grew stronger.

Unaware of how much time had passed, the orange light faded from Leyna's body. Looking up, Kiarra was rubbing her eyes. Before he could ask, the woman said, "I've reached my limit, Will. I think she's out of danger. That's the best we can hope for."

Millie walked up to them. "Jax and I have held out as long as we can, but one of the guards escaped. We need to move if we want a chance to leave here alive."

His concentration broken, Will's green light faded from Leyna's body. She breathed steadily and her heart pumped at a regular rhythm. He had no idea if he and Kiarra had managed to save her from the worst of it, but he couldn't confirm that until he had access to advanced medical equipment to check the state of her brain and other injuries.

A quick glance told him that Leyna's leg was still broken; the bone jutting out of her skin had to be painful. Will wasn't a medical doctor, but he needed to try to set it before moving her or she might lose the leg. He said to Millie, "Give me another minute. I need to set this." He motioned toward Leyna's upper body. "Hold her down, just in case. I can't afford for her to move or she may never walk on her own again."

Kiarra stood up slowly. "While you two do that, I'm going to check with Jaxton and the status of our helicopter."

Barely nodding, Will moved to Leyna's leg. The break was bad and setting the bone sticking out of her skin would be difficult. On top of that, Will had only helped set a broken bone as a student.

Taking a deep breath, he pushed aside his worry. The longer the jagged bone was outside the body, the greater chance of infection or any number of other problems.

However, before he could do more than study Leyna's broken bone, Millie sat across from him and pointed toward Leyna's head. "You hold her down. I'm trained as a field medic. And doctor you may be, but your expression tells me you don't know what the bloody hell you're doing."

He met Millie's eyes. "Have you set a broken bone like this before?"

Millie didn't miss a beat. "More than a few times. Now, hold her down. We don't have much time."

Not having a choice but to trust the woman he'd met the day before, Will moved to hold down Leyna's shoulders.

Millie took hold of Leyna's leg above and below the break. She murmured, "Three, two, one," and jerked the bone into place. Even unconscious, Leyna's body twitched. Without any drugs, he couldn't imagine the pain. It was a blessing she was out cold.

Ripping off his shirt, he pointed to Millie. "We need two straight sticks."

Millie raised an eyebrow, but went without another word. Her silence worried him. He would probably pay for it later.

However, he pushed aside his concerns to take advantage of his moment of privacy.

Will caressed Leyna's cheek. "After all of this trouble, you'd better wake up, Leyna Grunwald. And not just because I want you to live. No, we're also going to start over and I'm going to woo you all over again. I love you, Leyna."

Leyna remained silent, of course.

Millie raced back and picked up Will's shirt. "I'll do it."

As Millie used his shirt and the sticks to secure Leyna's leg, the faint whir of helicopter blades neared.

Millie tied her final knot and waved in the direction of the sound. "Our pilots will be here soon. I need to help Jax with the prisoners, so you're in charge of Petra. Be careful when you move her."

Nodding, Will looked back to Leyna's body. Her face was pale and her brows furrowed.

He would do anything to have her glare at him again.

Lightly brushing her jaw, he willed for her to be okay.

The sound of the helicopter grew louder and for once in his life, he was impatient to board one of the blasted things. Even if he had to dangle below the bloody machine to give Leyna enough room to be transported to a hospital, he'd do it. He'd spent too much time being angry at both himself and Leyna. All he wanted to do was have another chance.

Taking Leyna's hand, Will kept guard over his woman and hoped he had the opportunity to do so.

Millie Ward watched as the helicopter landed in a nearby clearing. She shouted to her brother at her side, "Did the pilots see any trouble coming our way?"

Jaxton shook his head. "Not yet. But with that guard missing, it's probable. We need to get out of here as soon as possible."

She looked down at the tan face of the elemental magic user who was probably the Earth Talent. "What are we going to do about her? As much as I hate to drug the poor dear, if she wakes up while we're in flight, she'll panic and possibly kill us all."

Kiarra leaned forward from Jaxton's other side. "We'll keep her sedated until we reach the UK. Once there, we'll talk with Marco and Darius and come up with a plan."

Darius Williams and Marco Alvarez were Elemental Masters. While they still had to keep their hands toward the east and west, respectively, to use their magic, they had far more training and knowledge about using elemental magic than most. They also had contacts and might be able to reach out to an Earth Master to help the woman learn to control her abilities.

Millie shifted her gaze to Kiarra. "Marco and Darius are great and all, but I think you'll be the biggest help, Kiarra."

Kiarra had once been a prisoner inside the AMT. She'd been experimented on and used as a guinea pig. At least, until Jaxton had rescued her.

Kiarra nodded. "I'm going to try my best. However, convincing Neena to keep me home for a while is going to be a chore."

Jaxton jumped in. "I don't know about that. If this woman is indeed the Earth Talent, Neena will do quite a bit to get her on DEFEND's side."

"I hope so," Kiarra answered. "This woman has probably gone through hell. I can't even imagine what the AMT researchers would've done to me if they'd known I was a Talent."

Jaxton wrapped an arm around Kiarra's shoulders and squeezed. "You can thank me for rescuing you later, love."

Kiarra rolled her eyes just as the helicopter touched down. Jaxton waved toward the prisoners tied up on the ground. "I need one of the pilots to help me. Kiarra, go fetch one of them. Millie, tell Evans to bring your friend."

Without a word, Millie raced back to Will Evans.

The man was holding Petra gently and stroking her cheek. Millie hesitated a second. Only because the pair would never have a chance to hash things out if they didn't get Petra to a hospital ASAP did Millie jog the rest of the way up to them. "Come. The helicopter is waiting."

Will delicately maneuvered Petra into his arms and stood up. Trusting him to follow, Millie headed back toward the helicopter.

Jaxton already had most of the prisoners inside the chopper. Millie climbed in and turned to help Will guide Petra inside. Once Will was sitting down on the ground, he leaned Petra against his chest with her legs straight in front of her. No doubt, the ride would jar her legs, but at least they would be somewhat stable, especially with Will's long legs on either side of hers.

Kiarra sat in the corner seat with the elemental earth user leaning against her. Four prisoners were tied up and stashed toward the back. Jaxton loaded the last one and climbed in. Shutting the door, the chopper took off.

As they started moving, Millie's gut told her it'd been too easy.

Peering out the window, she didn't see anything. Nor did she until the helicopter lurched and Millie nearly lost her seat. "What the bloody hell was that?"

Jaxton put his finger to his ear and listened to the pilots before relaying the information. "There are two helicopters pursuing us. That was a warning shot."

Millie frowned. "They wouldn't shoot us down, though, because the woman is too valuable. Still, what's the plan, brother?"

He looked to Kiarra. "I know you're close to burnout, but do you have a few shots of fire left in you?"

Kiarra answered, "It's not like I have a choice. Still, I need to know where before I attempt it. Once I pass out, I won't be a help to anyone."

Jaxton turned and made his way to the cockpit to ask for their pursuers' positions. Millie looked to Kiarra. "Are you sure you can handle this, Kiarra? You being unconscious isn't ideal."

"I know, but I'm the only one with any sort of combat magic. I think in the future, I'm going to require Neena to have two or three magic users on each high-profile mission."

Before Millie could reply, Jaxton was back. "There's a helicopter on each side. They keep switching who is closer and who is behind. Probably to avoid both being hit."

Kiarra smiled. "Well, the tactic isn't going to make much difference for my fire. They clearly don't understand how elemental magic is fueled by particles in the air."

Jaxton replied, "Exactly. I'm guessing they don't have much experience with elemental magic in combat operations."

Kiarra slid out of her seat and rearranged the magic user at her side. "But I need your touch, Jaxton, or I'm not going to be able to do much more than one blast of fire."

Jaxton moved to Kiarra's side and looked over his shoulder. Just as he opened his mouth, the helicopter jerked to the side. Both of them smacked against one of the helicopter's doors before regaining their balance.

Millie looked around and spotted a rope. Tossing it at the pair, she said, "I never thought I'd be telling my brother this, but tie yourselves up. Just keep the kinky stuff for later."

Jaxton sighed and secured both himself and Kiarra before tying the other end of the rope to a bar on the side. "I hope everyone is strapped in."

Millie finished securing the cargo net in the back portion, to ensure the prisoners wouldn't fall to their deaths. A quick glance showed that Will was in a chair with Petra turned to the side. Her legs were balancing on the arm of the adjacent chair. While not ideal, it would do.

Strapping herself in, Millie nodded. "Go get them, you two."

Kiarra opened the side door and wind whipped through the small space. It was bloody freezing.

Squinting her eyes, Millie watched as Kiarra summoned a flame to her palm and shot it out the side. No sooner had she attempted to repeat the process when a mixture of rain and snow pelted sideways, into the helicopter. It wasn't winter; something was off.

The helicopter rolled to the side for a split second before righting itself. Kiarra banged her head against the doorframe and Jaxton had to hold tight to keep from falling.

"Kiarra? Are you okay?" Millie asked.

Just as Kiarra was about to reply, the helicopter lurched again. This time, Jaxton's ironclad grip kept them in place.

He poked his head outside for a second and quickly treated. "They're switching positions again, love. It's now or never. Are you ready?"

"As much as I'll ever be." Kiarra rubbed her temple a second before standing tall. "I wish there was another way to stop them. Regardless of who they are, I hate killing anyone."

Millie understood the feeling. "But think of it this way—if you don't, they'll kill us. And then the whole world could die. I'd say it's necessary in this case."

Closing her eyes, Kiarra summoned a flame on each hand. As they dance, the light reflected off the metal bits of the helicopter.

A small part of Millie was jealous that she didn't have any sort of magical powers. But then she pushed the feeling away. Having magic was both a burden and a curse, as she'd seen with both Kiarra and Millie's eldest brother, Garrett.

The reflections vanished as Kiarra directed one stream of flame from her hands to outside the helicopter. A second later, another stream swam through the air, out of Millie's sight.

Too bad she was strapped to the seat and couldn't watch it make its mark.

Something finally exploded behind them and Millie's helicopter veered off to the left, hard. Petra slid to the side, but Will tightened his grip and kept the woman in place.

As the commotion calmed down, Millie noted that the snow, rain, and high winds died.

Millie's intuition said there was a connection.

Jaxton shut the side door and maneuvered Kiarra to an empty seat. While Kiarra was still conscious, the dark rings under her eyes and her pale face spoke volumes.

Looking to her brother, Millie asked, "Did you get both of them?"

"No," Jaxton answered. "But as soon as Kiarra hit one, the other retreated." He paused and put a finger to his ear. "The pilot confirms the retreat and is getting the hell out of here."

As Jaxton put an arm around Kiarra's shoulder and drew her against his side, Kiarra closed her eyes. Everyone fell silent; the whir of the blades above was almost relaxing in the aftermath.

Millie used the time to run through every *Feiru* legend and myth she'd heard from childhood to the present. There was something familiar about the sudden shift in the weather, but she couldn't quite pinpoint it.

Whatever it was, Millie sensed it would cause DEFEND a major headache in the future.

CHAPTER ELEVEN

Two days later, Will sat inside a room in DEFEND's infirmary in northern England and stroked Leyna's hand. She remained unconscious, but he wanted her to know he was at her side.

The doctors had assured him there wasn't any swelling in Leyna's brain and that the break in her leg would mostly heal clean. They'd also issued a warning against any more magical healing since it was unknown whether too much of it could harm a patient. Apparently, all records had been lost in the great purge of *Feiru*-related information in the 1950s.

If Will had anything to say about it, he would help rediscover the limits of his own power.

But that didn't help him in the present. Neither doctor had guaranteed anything about Leyna waking up without any brain damage. He hated being powerless to change that.

He murmured, "Come on, woman. We wasted two years. Let's not waste any more time."

Leyna remained motionless except for the rise and fall of her chest.

With a sigh, Will adjusted his position in the chair. He debated telling Leyna another memory from their past before their lives had separated when the door clicked open. Turning, he spotted Neena Chatterjee. He growled out, "What do you want?"

Neena entered, shut the door, and tilted her head. "You should be happy to see me, William. After all, I am a very busy woman."

Remember she's in charge here. Remember. Taking a deep inhalation, Will forced his voice to be less hostile. "Then would you care to tell me why you're honoring us with your presence?"

Neena skipped to the other side of Leyna's bed. "A bit better, although if you add 'your highness' to the end, it might win you some favors."

Will gritted his teeth. Neena had visited once before, when they'd first landed. She'd merely said, "She's still the living dead," before disappearing.

Millie had stressed the importance of remaining on Neena's good side. However, his patience was quickly evaporating.

Shrugging, Neena placed a hand on Leyna's forehead. "I think you'd enjoy Leyna-slash-Petra's dreams. She really should pick a name and stick with it."

Ignoring the latter statement, Will dared to ask, "How would you know about her dreams?"

"Because I'm a Dream-Speaker, of course." Neena lowered her voice. "Recently, I've needed a few cold showers after talking with Little Miss Slash here."

Will's eye twitched. "Her dreams mean nothing if she's trapped in them forever."

Neena grinned. "Considering they're sexy and feature yourself, you might approve."

The woman's words pumped up his ego a notch, but Will pushed it aside. "Maybe you should stop violating people's privacy."

"I'm not so sure about that. Call me 'your highness', and I just might be able to persuade her to wake up."

Will wanted to tell the woman to bugger off, but Millie's warning replayed inside his head: *Neena can become your greatest ally, but she can also become your worst enemy. Tread lightly.*

He forced his voice to be even. "How?" Neena merely raised her brows and Will resisted sighing. "How, your highness?"

"Now, that wasn't so hard, was it?" Neena stood a little taller. "As for how, watch and be amazed, lad. You're going to owe me a few favors for this."

Neena closed her eyes and stood silently. Will squeezed Leyna's hand in his. Each second that passed only irritated him. If Neena was giving him false hope, then he didn't bloody well care who she was or what she could do, he would find a way to tie her up and get some answers. Who knew what other powers the woman was hiding from him; there might be one to help his Leyna.

~~~

Petra stood inside her old apartment, the one she had shared with Will until two years ago. The secondhand couch took up most of the living room, with a small TV and stereo near the front. Five paces away was the small kitchen. Beyond was the tiny bedroom that was barely big enough for their bed.

Two graduate students couldn't afford anything better in the greater London area. Yet as she surveyed the small space, each slightly used item brought back the memories of comfort and happiness with Will.

God, she'd loved him so much. No one had been able to make her laugh with a corny joke as much as him. Not to mention he'd always tried to tickle her when she least expected it. Back then, Petra had been the more serious of the two.

She should mourn the loss of the easygoing version of Will. And yet, Petra loved the more discerning, determined man he'd become. Both of them had changed, and in an odd way, they might fit better than before.

If only she could find him.

Petra had tried countless times to leave the apartment. However, every time she exited the door, it only put her back into the small set of rooms again. Maybe she had died after all and existing in the apartment was her personal version of hell.

No. She didn't want to be dead. Not just because her brother's life would be in jeopardy without her help, but also because she needed to tell Will how she felt. Kissing him back in the helicopter wasn't enough; Petra wanted to state her feelings without leaving any doubt.

A small part of her worried Will hadn't made it out of Hong Kong alive. But given what Petra knew of Millie Ward, her friend had probably ensured everyone's escape. Petra only hoped the elemental earth user had survived or Petra's sacrifice would've been in vain.

Just as she plopped down on the couch, there was a knock on the door. *That's new.*

Making her way to the door, she looked out of the peephole. Neena Chatterjee's smiling face winked at her. "Let me in, lovely. I'm here to save the day."

Opening the door, Petra frowned. "Neena?"

The woman snapped her fingers and a multicolored cape settled around her shoulders. "Much better. Now I'm ready to save the day."

Dismissing the woman's eccentricities, Petra asked, "Are you dead, too?"

"Dead? No, my dear. I'd need a much better outfit than this. Death would require a fancy sari. Or maybe a ballgown. Oooh, or some combination of the two."

Petra took a deep inhalation and released it before daring another question. "If you're saving the day, then does that mean you're here to save me?"

Neena snapped her fingers. "Right-o, my dear. Although, before I do the deed, we need to chat about a few things. As you're a mercenary, I'm sure you understand that while I could do this for free, it's not necessarily in my best interests."

Petra's respect for Neena went up a notch. "What are the terms?"

"Straight to the point. I like that." Neena waltzed into the room and perched her behind on the back of the couch. "While joining DEFEND and having your cleverness and skills available is a must, I first need to ask why you want to be saved in the first place. Let's hope you don't give the wrong answer."

Given what little she knew of Neena, Petra had no idea what might be considered a wrong answer. Petra would simply go with the truth. "I need to tell Will something."

"Aw, the handsome researcher. He has a surprise or two in store for us in the future." Neena leaned forward. "The only question is are you a part of his future or not?"

Petra didn't miss a beat. "I hope so."

Neena clapped her hands together. "Good answer. Both of you on my side will make things that much more brilliant."

Petra opened her mouth to ask Neena to elaborate, but the woman snapped her fingers and Petra was pulled toward the door. As she floated down the hallway toward a black nothingness, Petra wondered how many latent abilities Neena possessed. Just as that thought formed, a blazing light flashed and warmth spread over her body.

126

The next second she heard Will's voice in the bright, vast space she floated in. "Well, what happened, Neena? You're back but Leyna isn't."

Neena's voice filled Petra's ears. "Maybe she just needs true love's kiss."

Will growled. "Stop with the bloody games. Why is Leyna still unconscious?"

Petra wanted to shout that she was listening, but she could do nothing but float in the brightness. Neena spoke up again. "Oh, I think she's listening. And if I'm correct, which I always am, she'll wake up with a kiss."

"If you're out to make me a fool, Neena Chatterjee, you'll make an enemy."

"Believe me, William, you do not want me as an enemy." Neena clicked her tongue. "Now, kiss the woman."

There was a beat of silence before warm, soft lips descended on hers. In the next second, her heart jumped and she was yanked upward.

~~~

Will gently kissed Leyna's silky lips. To be honest, he felt like a fool following Neena's childish games. But if there was even the slightest chance it would help his Leyna, Will would dance around a bonfire naked if it meant his woman would wake up.

Lightly tucking her hair behind an ear, Will debated ending the kiss when Leyna's lips moved below his. It wasn't more than a twitch at first. But as he licked her lower lip, Leyna nipped his upper one a second later. Pulling back, he met Leyna's green eyes. "Leyna."

"Will," she croaked.

He cupped her face with his hands and stroked his thumbs against her cheeks. "Did you really come back to me? I'm afraid this is just a dream or some kind of vision."

She gave a weak smile. "If this is a dream or vision, then the pain in my leg feels damn real."

He grimaced. "I'm sorry, Leyna. Millie and I tried the best we could. But the break needed surgery and we didn't arrive as soon as we should have. The pain is partially my fault."

Leyna's brows furrowed. "I don't care about my leg. I'm alive. What happened?"

Will glanced up, but Neena had disappeared. Not caring how the crazy woman had done it, Will took advantage of their privacy. "First, tell me who I am and what you've been doing for the last few years."

"You're Dr. William Evans and I was a mercenary."

"Good," he answered. "I'll give you more tests later, but I don't think you're brain damaged."

Petra growled. "I'm fine. Just bloody tell me what happened."

Her threat only strengthened his relief at her condition. "We arrived in one piece." He recounted him healing her as well as Kiarra blowing up the helicopter. He added, "But all that matters is that we're safe and you're awake. I was afraid that I'd lost you again, Leyna."

"Will, please call me Petra."

"But why, love? Leyna is such a pretty name."

"Because that's not who I am anymore. I have something to tell you, but only if you accept me as Petra, the badass mercenary-slash-scientist."

He traced her jaw. "Of course I accept you. If calling you Petra is what it takes to win you over, I will do that and more."

She raised her brows. "I sense a 'but.' Be honest with me, Will. What is it?"

He caressed her cheek. "The mercenary part may not be in your future." Leyna—no, Petra—opened her mouth to reply, but he beat her to it. "It has nothing to do with me or my wishes, Petra. The doctor thinks you're going to limp for the rest of your life."

Petra placed a hand on his arm. "Then we need to find a way to ensure my brother's safety. Without me to look out for him, he'll get himself killed."

"I'm already working on that. Millie owed me a favor and I called it in."

She frowned. "But how? I haven't told her anything."

"Between the two of us, as well as a few other DEFEND members, we've figured out your brother is Dominick and the drug lord boss is Sean Reilly. Millie should be taking him down as we speak."

Petra attempted to sit up, but Will pushed gently against her shoulders to keep her in place. "You're not going anywhere. Deep down, you know that you're more of a liability right now than an asset."

Grunting, Petra relaxed against the bed. "Maybe. But I don't like the idea of owing Millie anything. If she survives the attempt, that is."

"Millie can take care of herself."

Skepticism flashed in her eyes. "Maybe."

Will growled. "Look, I've accepted your new name, so I need you to try and accept something as well. If you don't learn to trust me and others, we can't help you. More than that, we can't help DEFEND and avoid Neena Chatterjee's wrath."

Petra searched his eyes for a few seconds. "I trust you, Will."

129

He leaned down until his face was mere inches from hers. "Good. Now, what was it that you wanted to tell me?"

Holding his breath, Will waited for Petra's answer.

~~~

Petra stared into Will's brown eyes and debated telling him the truth. Sure, she'd wanted nothing more than to tell him of her feelings while she'd been stuck in that dream world. But with his scent and heat near, her heart rate increased and her palms started to sweat.

She was afraid of rejection.

Get a grip, Brandt. Take what you want or walk away. Stop dawdling. With a deep inhalation, the words rushed out on her exhale. "What I wanted to say is that I've never stopped loving you, Will. I know there's a shit-ton of things to discuss and it will take time to fully become reacquainted. But over the last few days, I've seen enough of the man I loved to know I still love him. Changed or not, I want to try again."

Will smiled and Petra's body relaxed. "Good, because I'd already made my mind up to pursue you, Petra. You wanting the same thing will make things easier."

An almost foreign urge to tease him filled her body. "Oh, so if I hadn't been on board, what would you have done?"

He traced the curve of her cheek. "Lots of touching." He leaned down and nuzzled his whisker-covered cheek against hers. The stubble sent a little thrill through her body. She barely heard his whisper, "Not to mention using your fondness for my stubble to soften you more."

"What else?"

Moving his head until his eyes met hers again and his lips were less than an inch away, he answered, "Then I would kiss and tease you until you begged for more."

Heat coursed through her body and Petra all but forgot about the pain in her leg. "I rather think I'll be the one teasing you until you begged for more."

He raised an eyebrow. "Oh, really?"

"I may end up limping for the rest of my life, but I still have a few tricks up my sleeve." She grinned at the heat in his gaze. "And now I'll have you thinking of what they may be until my leg is healed enough to use them."

Will gently kissed her and murmured, "I have a few fantasies to share while we wait. If anything, you'll be the impatient one."

Petra laughed. "You've just issued a challenge, Will. Even in our former lives, that was dangerous. I'm out to win."

"So am I."

As they stared into one another's gaze, Petra raised a hand and lightly caressed his jaw. "In all seriousness, I never thought I'd have this chance again with you, Will. Let's promise right here and now to discuss anything that happens. I should've done so two years ago, but while I can't turn back the clock, I can make a fresh start."

"Not a fresh start, love. We're just righting ourselves after a small bump in the road."

Petra had no idea how she deserved the man above her. "I love you, William Evans."

"Just as I love you, Petra, er, which last name are you using now?"

"Brandt."

His eyes grew tender. "I love you, Petra Brandt."

At Will using her full new name, Petra ran her hand into his hair. "Then kiss me, Will."

Lowering his head, his lips moved slowly at first before Petra opened her mouth. With each stroke of his tongue, Will melted her heart a little more.

The man she had betrayed seemed to have forgiven and accepted her. Petra only hoped they had a future. Because with each claim on her mouth, Will was ruining her for all other men. Sexy and smart were a rare package, and this time, Petra was going to fight with everything she had to keep him.

CHAPTER TWELVE

A week later, Will pushed Petra in a wheelchair down the hall to one of the small meeting rooms. As he tried to maneuver the bloody thing around the corner, Petra sighed and said, "You should've let me use the crutches."

He grunted. "Not yet. Even the doctor suggested a few more days off your feet to give you the best chance at healing." Will made the turn and headed toward the entry to the meeting room. "And the only reason I'm taking you to this blasted meeting is because Neena requested it."

She clicked her tongue. "And because I wanted to go. Sometimes your protectiveness is endearing, but at other times, it annoys the hell out of me. Once I'm healed and out of this chair, I'm going to be a lot less complacent. I hope you're ready."

He lowered his voice for dramatic effect. "Oh, I'm more than ready, love. Taking care of you is nice, but I look forward to matching wits."

Petra snorted and Will bit back a smile. Challenging each other had definitely become one of their favorite pastimes and he couldn't wait to start fighting them out.

The door opened to reveal Millie Ward. Despite the bruise on her cheek, the woman was smiling. Petra was the first to ask, "What happened to you?"

Millie shrugged. "Sean Reilly was a little bit of a challenge."

Will beat Petra to the punch. "You took care of him?"

Millie winked. "But of course. He may have been a challenge, but his cockiness was his downfall. Well, and his weakness for pretty women." She motioned behind her. "But enough about that bastard. I brought you back a surprise."

A tall man with the same brown hair and green eyes as Petra walked forward. He smiled at Petra. "Sis."

"Dom." Petra moved to stand up, but Will pushed down on her shoulder. He eyed Dom as he asked, "You seem pretty happy despite how much shit you've put your sister through. I'm wondering if it's even wise to have you here at all."

Petra grabbed his hand and he met her eyes as she said, "Stop it, Will."

He shook his head. "No. You gave up your life for him. Looking at him, he doesn't seem the least bit grateful."

Before either Petra or Dom could reply, Millie stepped between Petra and Dom. "Now, now, we all need to play nice. Neena invited Dominick here, and her word is final."

Will growled. "Then maybe I should take it up with Neena."

Millie replied, "You'll have your chance soon enough. She's due to arrive any minute. If you're clever, and I think you are, you'll let your girlfriend have her reunion with her brother. Otherwise, you might be sleeping alone on a couch somewhere."

Petra's voice filled his ears. "She's right. I'm drawing a line at your protectiveness."

Will knew he was being unrealistic, but he hated how much Petra's brother took advantage of her. He'd just have to have a chat with the man later. It was about time for Dominick to hold his own as a man. "Then tell Millie to move. She's the one blocking you, not me."

Millie snorted. "I suppose I am."

Millie stepped aside and Will met Dom's gaze again. They measured each other up a second before the other man walked to his sister and crouched down. "Hey, sis. Long time, no see."

~~~

Petra tapped her fingers against her thigh and debated how to handle her brother.

For all that she'd asked to see him, she was torn between kicking him in the shin with her good leg and engulfing him in a hug. Will was right that she'd coddled him over the years. Not that she wanted to admit it.

Okay, maybe she would in private. She had promised to be honest with Will.

Compromising, Petra put out a hand and Dom took it. She cleared her throat. "I'm glad you're alive, but if you ever go making backdoor deals with drug dealers or other powerful foes, I'm going to let you rot, Dominick Brandt."

The corner of Dom's mouth ticked up. "How do you expect to do that with your leg in a cast?"

Will hissed out, "She earned that cast saving another woman's life."

Dom looked up to Will. The tension radiating between the two was giving her a headache. "I'm starting to think working on my own as a mercenary again might be the best option."

Both men said, "No."

Will blinked. "It looks like we agree on something."

Petra waved her hands. "Hello, I'm the one supposed to be having the reunion."

Dom grinned at her. "Oh, Millie has a grand plan for a reunion party next week."

Millie tsked. "Thanks for ruining the surprise, younger Brandt twin."

Looking between Millie and Dom, Petra frowned. "Since when are you two so friendly?"

Millie answered, "Hey, when you survive a life or death situation, you tend to bond. Maybe the three of us can form our own little DEFEND unit. Then I wouldn't be stuck following my brother everywhere."

Jaxton's dry voice came from behind Petra. "I thought I was keeping you alive. If you want to bloody get yourself killed, go for it."

Millie stuck out her tongue. "I just took down the head of a drug cartel. Give me a little credit, Jax."

Kiarra's voice jumped in and Petra looked over her shoulder as she said, "I'm starting to think there should be a new DEFEND rule—siblings should be separated. It would save us a whole hell of a lot of time."

Millie pointed a finger at Kiarra. "You're just jealous. I think because your sister is badass and out doing high-priority missions with her boyfriend, not to mention your brother is locked up, you feel as if you're missing out."

Jaxton growled out, "Enough." At the authority in his tone, everyone fell quiet and he carried on. "Neena will be here soon. I suggest we settle around the table or she might jump and expect us to help her bodysurf."

Petra bit her lip. She would love to see Jaxton and Will helping Neena surf over their hands. "Do you know what it's about?"

Kiarra answered, "Probably about the Earth Talent, although with Neena, who knows."

Petra met Will's gaze. He'd been studying the woman's blood in between his bedside vigils. "Is there something you haven't told me, Will?"

Will shook his head. "Most of the tests are still running and will take some time to complete. Unless they've taken her off the rowan-berry juice, I have no idea what Neena wants to discuss."

The elemental earth user's name was Naiyana Chaiket, but preferred to be called Yana. Apart from revealing her name and the fact she was Thai-born and raised near Chiang Mai until age thirteen by parents she wouldn't talk about, the woman had been quiet. Neena's orders were to not take advantage of the woman, which included no detailed questioning. The rowan-berry juice was only being administered to keep her from using her powers until a skilled earth user arrived to help her learn to control her abilities.

Eyeing her brother, Petra then looked to Millie. "Are you sure Neena wants Dom here?"

Millie bobbed her head. "Of course. I'm not about to get onto Neena's shit list by bringing strangers to a super-top secret meeting without her permission."

Before she could ask any more questions, a cheery voice boomed out, "Let's get this party started!"

Taking a deep inhalation, Petra turned her face toward Neena. The woman wore a form-fitting, black party dress without any straps. Her hair was twisted up into a fancy hairdo. Neon-colored stars dangled from her ears.

Will was the first to speak up. "May I ask why you're wearing a dress?" Neena raised her brows and Will gritted out, "Your highness?"

Neena beamed. "I wanted to look pretty. Thanks for noticing." She waved a hand at the chairs arranged around a table.

"Sit down. The sooner we're done with the boring stuff, the sooner we can crank up the music and start dancing."

A quick glance at Dom and Petra saw her brother frowning in confusion. As Will wheeled her past Dom, Petra whispered, "Just go with it. I'd suggest keeping quiet until you better understand the way things work here."

"If you say so," Dom muttered.

Considering her brother's penchant for not following advice, Petra only hoped Dom didn't do too much damage.

As everyone settled around the table, Petra waited to see what would happen.

~ ~ ~

Will sat beside Petra's wheelchair and took her hand in his. Keeping one eye on her no-good brother, he listened as Neena started to speak.

"Let me start with the obvious—because we're fabulous, we have three of the four Talents on our side. You may think the next step is finding the fourth one. However, you're wrong. There is a selfish, greedy dimwit we need to take care of first."

Neena leaned against the wall and took out a mobile phone. As she fiddled with it, Jaxton chimed in. "Care to expand on that?"

Putting up a finger to signal to wait, Will debated pinning Neena up against the wall and shaking some answers out of her. Not only did he have research to do, he needed to talk with Petra in private about her brother. Will was clever enough to know Petra wouldn't take any edicts well. However, he needed to find a way to prevent Dom from taking advantage of his sister.

Just as he moved to stand up, Neena met his gaze. "I wouldn't suggest it, researcher man. The fate of the world is in my hands. You just need to be patient."

Jaxton's terse voice answered, "Neena, get to the point already. We each have a million things to do. Watching you play with your phone isn't one of them."

Neena sniffed. "Only because I love you, Jaxy, will I let your tone slide this time. Eventually, your impatience will get you into trouble." Jaxton opened his mouth to reply, but Neena beat him to it. "Any-who, a woman is collecting *Feiru* with latent abilities. She's completely unoriginal and calls herself the Collector. You all need to find her."

Neena took two steps to the door and Will quickly asked, "That's it?"

She shrugged. "I can't always be holding your hands. Step up and figure it out yourself."

The DEFEND leader clapped her hands and music blared from somewhere. Before anyone could blink, she rushed out of the room and slammed the door behind her.

The music instantly died down.

Everyone looked at each other before settling on Jaxton. The DEFEND commander cleared his throat. "Just because Neena didn't spell things out doesn't mean we can't accomplish the mission. Kiarra and I know someone who has had a run-in with this woman and will talk with them for more information. Millie, study the transcripts and videos of Giovanni's interrogations to see what you can find about the woman who kidnapped those three volunteers."

Millie tilted her head. "Why don't I just talk to him?"

Jaxton didn't miss a beat. "I don't trust you alone with him and I don't have the time to make sure you behave."

"I can behave, Jaxton," Millie said as she placed a hand on her hip. "I just took down a drug lord.

Jaxton answered, "Maybe, but I'm not going to chance it. You have your orders. Follow them."

Millie reluctantly nodded as she muttered a few choice words. Jaxton then looked to Will. "How long until your preliminary results come back on the Earth Talent?"

Will leaned forward. "Any time now. But I'm not sure how that's going to help. Latent abilities and elemental abilities are two very different things."

Petra spoke up. "Maybe and maybe not. If we compare the genome sequences of the elemental earth user with yours, we can see if the two overlap or both have unique sequences not found in humans or *Feiru* with no known abilities. If so, we might be able to devise something to target and temporarily neutralize the ability. If the Collector doesn't have her coerced army to protect her, she will become a much easier target."

Will squeezed Petra's hand in his. "I told you the research and mercenary experiences work well together."

She smiled. "Then you won't have any objections to me helping you with your research."

It was on the tip of Will's tongue to say Petra needed to rest, but the eagerness in her eyes stayed the words. Since Petra may never be able to work a field mission again, bringing her into his research would be the first baby steps toward accepting her eventual fate with DEFEND.

Besides, it meant he could spend even more time with his Petra. "As long as we're partners and you don't try to take over, I might be persuaded to work with you."

Petra winked. "I can't make any promises, but I'll try."

As they stared at one another, Will couldn't help but reach out a finger to trace her cheek. "If I use your stubbornness and competitiveness against you, we'll have things figured out within the week."

"Save your flirting for later," Jaxton jumped in. "I may check in with you two every few hours to ensure you're focused and not distracted."

Kiarra lightly slapped his arm. "Jaxton. Give them a break. Imagine if we'd been apart for two years."

Wrapping an arm around Kiarra's waist, Jaxton murmured, "Don't even mention that."

Jaxton lowered his head to kiss his woman when Dom blurted out, "What about me?"

Never blinking, Jaxton met Dom's gaze. "You'll be training. I don't know why Neena insisted you be here. But until that reason becomes clear, you'll be under constant watch."

"Hey, I'm not running for my life and I have somewhere to sleep." Dom shrugged. "That's good enough for me."

Petra warned, "Dom."

He met Petra's eyes. "I'm just being honest, sis. You already know my skills. I'll just keep a low profile until the rest of the gang here understands them as well."

Will wondered how in the hell Dom had survived as a mercenary. Maybe his nonchalance was a distraction, but Will would need to ask Petra about it later.

Jaxton grunted. "Fine. Kiarra and I will escort Dominick to the training area. The rest of you, get to work."

Giving a thumbs-up, Millie walked briskly out of the room.

Will stood up and gripped the handles of the wheelchair. He pushed, but Petra raised a hand. "I should talk with Dom some more."

Jaxton's voice cut off Will's reply. "Not now, Petra. I need you to work with Will. Any insights into latent abilities or elemental ones will be paramount to our success. You can talk with your brother later, if he survives training without any reprimands."

Will's respect for Jaxton raised a hair. "He's right. Some of the results should be ready. Since you've been talking about how much you miss working on research, let's get right to it. Unless you need to rest."

Petra rolled her eyes. "I'm not any more tired than when you asked me half an hour ago. Let's go. The sooner I see your results, the sooner I can point out the things you missed."

He pushed Petra's wheelchair out of the room. "I haven't even glanced at it."

"You're so distracted by my welfare, all it would take is showing a little cleavage and you would forget everything else." Petra smiled.

"Not true. And I'll prove it to you."

Petra raised an eyebrow. "Is that a challenge?"

"Yes. But let's make it more interesting, shall we? Whoever makes the greatest discovery gets to have their fantasy played out."

She raised her brows. "And just what kind of fantasy are you talking about? One where I meet the actor of my dreams?" Petra replied, her voice tinged with humor.

Will pierced her with a glare. "The only man in your dreams should be me."

She clicked her tongue. "Someone's jealous."

He gripped the handles of her wheelchair tighter. "Bloody right I am. Only because of your leg have I not tried to get you naked and at my mercy."

A flush crept up Petra's cheeks. "Keep your voice down. Anyone can hear you."

"So? If they don't know by now that you're my woman, then they aren't very intelligent."

He turned her chair into the room he used for his research. Turning on the light, he kicked the door closed and moved to crouch down in front of Petra. Tracing her lower lip with his forefinger, he murmured, "Maybe I should remind you of why you want me and only me."

Heat flared in her eyes. "Maybe you should."

He leaned closer. "I love that you don't hesitate with me."

Placing a hand on his cheek, she answered, "I'm just trying to make up for lost time."

"Good answer," he growled before taking her lips in a rough kiss.

Careful not to bump her leg, Will tilted his head and swept his tongue into her mouth. Her small moan vibrated against his tongue and shot straight to his cock.

All too soon, Petra pulled back. They both breathed heavily as they gazed into one another's eyes. Will asked, "Why did you stop?"

"Because I have a competition to win."

Laying his forehead against hers, he murmured, "Surely the results can wait a bleeding minute."

"You have a choice—talk about my brother, as I know you want to do, or kiss me again."

He sighed. "All I want to say about your brother is let him stand on his own two feet. If he can't do that at his age, then he should choose a different line of work."

Petra shook her head. "Did it ever occur to you that I was going to do that anyway?"

"He took advantage of you, love. I don't want him to have the chance to do it again."

"And I'm a big enough person to realize what I did wrong before."

He frowned. "Just like that?"

143

Petra shrugged one shoulder. "Nearly dying has put a few things into perspective. I don't intend to waste time trying to save everyone at my own expense again. I love my brother and would still charge into battle to save him if his life truly depended on it, but I'm no longer going to watch his every action. I need to live for myself as well."

Will rubbed his hand up and down Petra's upper thighs. "I hope there's some room for me, too."

She remained silent and Will gently clutched her thighs. If Petra was trying to tease him, he didn't like it.

Smiling, Petra kissed him quickly. "Of course."

Growling, he moved his hands to her waist. "Then why take so bloody long to say so?"

She grinned. "Because it's fun. I like making you squirm."

At the humor dancing in her eyes, Will's irritation eased a fraction. "It's nice to see you opening up, Petra. I love all of you, but it's good to see some of your humor is still intact. I think we're going to need it in the future."

Placing her hands over his, she answered, "Don't be so negative. Look at everything Jaxton, Millie, and the others have accomplished since we met them. I think Neena has a chance at winning."

"I'm not sure whether to be glad we're on the same side or scared at relying on that woman," Will muttered.

"Well, she'll definitely be scary if we don't get to work soon. Maybe I'll find the answers we need today and then I can ask for my fantasy."

"But your leg—"

Petra waved a hand. "There are plenty of ways to work around that. Besides, it barely hurts at all anymore." He frowned and she added, "It's the truth. If you won't believe anything else, then believe this—I'm done with keeping secrets from you. I love you and don't want to lose you again. If the pain in my leg becomes too much, I'll tell you."

Searching her eyes, his desire to protect battled with the honesty of her words. "I don't want to lose you either. I guess it just means I need to find a solution first. That way I can postpone the fantasy until after the cast comes off."

She smiled with mischief in her gaze. "If you think I'm waiting that many weeks to see you naked, I may have to jump you when you wake up in the morning. A little skin-to-skin friction should melt all of that steely resolve."

He nipped her lip. "If you lay on the bed and let me be on top, then I might be willing to negotiate."

Will took her mouth in a rough, quick kiss. Sooner than he liked, he pulled away. The sight of Petra's reddened lips only reminded him of what he needed to win to have those beauties caressing every inch of his body. Just the image of her plump, warm lips around his cock made him a little hard.

Petra whispered, "Why did you stop?"

He chuckled. "What happened to staying on Neena's good side and doing our work?"

"I'm to be the responsible one again?"

Standing up and holding out his hands, Will answered, "Come here, love."

She took his hands and he gently pulled at the same time as Petra balanced on one foot. Picking her up at the waist, he sat her down on the desk so he could stand between her legs. With one possessive hand on her arse and the other on the nape of her neck, he murmured, "Just show how much you love me with a kiss and then we'll get to work. I may even give you a five minute head start."

Petra tilted her head. "I can't imagine you giving me an advantage."

"Why not? It just gives me the chance to memorize every line and curve of your body while I watch you." He nibbled her lip. "I will never tire of looking at my woman."

Petra's breath hitched and her eyes turned wet. "I keep thinking this is all a dream and I'll wake up alone, without you."

He brushed the hair from her face. "I'm not going anywhere. And even if this were a dream, I'd search high and low until I found you again. You fill an emptiness in my very soul, Petra Brandt. I took you for granted once, but I'm never doing it again."

"Kiss me, Will."

Lowering his head, Will slipped his tongue between her warm, soft lips. He'd barely stroked inside before Petra threaded her fingers through his hair and stroked back.

Pulling her body closer to his, Will wasn't about to screw up his second chance.

Hell, he couldn't believe she'd given it to him. Deepening the kiss, he took his time showing Petra how much he loved her with his mouth. No matter if he had to jump out of a helicopter to save her, Will was going to fight to keep Petra Brandt.

He just needed to stop the bloody curse first or they'd never grow old together.

EPILOGUE

Will adjusted the focus on his microscope. He was about to jot down his latest findings when his computer chirped. Lifting his head, he met Petra's gaze. "It's done."

Since Petra sat at the desk, she was the first to click the mouse. Data and graphs popped up on the screen. Will moved to stand behind her. After a cursory scan, he muttered, "Bloody hell. You were right."

Leaning her head back against his abdomen, she replied, "Glad you can admit that. It means I won."

Placing his hands on her shoulders, he gently kneaded. "Forget about the bloody competition for a second. After months of sequencing individuals inside DEFEND and compiling the data, the computer algorithm was finally able to pinpoint the genome sequence in those with latent abilities." He tapped the screen. "That's it."

The blinking line consisted of a mixture of the letters A, C, G, and T, which spelled out the unique code of instructions used inside every cell.

Petra placed one of her hands over his on her shoulder and squeezed. "I think you missed the other half of the big news on the screen. Look at the list of subjects positive for that sequence."

Will glanced over to the right. Several of those with latent abilities, including himself, were listed. Then he spotted a specific name and frowned. "Your brother."

"I wonder why he hasn't displayed any sort of special power yet. Considering he's around Kiarra and Yana often enough, the proximity to two Talents should bring it out."

Will grunted. "It's more likely he's hiding it from us. I know he's your brother, but there's a reason Jaxton hasn't let him out of the training sessions yet to help Millie gather information on the Collector—Dom hasn't earned anyone's trust yet."

Petra sighed. "Can we discuss Dom and his issues later? After all, we just made a pretty damn big discovery, even if we haven't managed to complete our research on the first-borns and their elemental magic." She slid from the chair and moved to lean against Will's chest. "But before we share the news and Neena makes us test every known member of DEFEND, I think you need to pay up."

Will wrapped his arms around Petra's waist. "I'm not so sure about that. After all, you only discovered part of what's needed to win the bet. Not only do we still need to identify the exact sequence for first-borns, we also need to figure out what to do with the identified sequences. Waving around a piece of paper at the Collector's coerced army isn't going to stop them or suspend their abilities."

"Give it some time. Neena has provided us with resources beyond our wildest dreams."

"Only because she uses her foresight on the stock market," Will grumbled.

She lightly slapped his chest. "Can you stop being grumpy and just humor me? We've earned the right to celebrate this discovery before being bogged down with even more work."

He hugged Petra tighter against him. "I'm just being honest."

Her gaze turned mischievous as she moved a hand to the back of his neck and lightly brushed his nape with her fingers. The light touch sent a rush of heat through his body, straight to his cock. It took everything he had not to clear the desk of the computer equipment with one swoop and take Petra right then and there.

Her warm breath tickled his chin as she murmured, "I love your honesty." She kissed his jaw. "But right now, I still say I won the bet and want to collect." She nibbled his earlobe. "What do you say?"

"We can debate whether you've won or not later."

"Will, I won—"

"We can play out your fantasy later. Right now, I need you."

Will lowered his head and kissed her.

~~~

Petra barely had time to open her mouth before Will claimed her lips. At his heady taste, she moaned and Will possessively gripped her ass cheeks. As he rocked her body against his erection, Petra pushed against his chest and gasped. "Take off your clothes. Now."

He nipped her neck and licked the sting with his tongue. "Such a demanding creature."

Not waiting for permission, she ripped open his shirt, the buttons flying every which way. At Will's sound of protest, she said, "That's why we have spares in the closet."

Shrugging out of his shirt, Will moved his hands to his pants. "Unless you want me to rip your clothes off, because I will, then get undressed."

Petra didn't waste time tearing off her shirt and wiggling out of her skirt.

Stepping out of the skirt, she couldn't help but smile. She had started wearing them most of the time because of easy access.

Will's warm hands at her shoulders, slipping off her bra straps, brought her back to the present. After sliding them off, he reached around and unhooked her bra without trouble. The bra fell to the ground and Will waggled his eyebrows. Petra laughed. "You're so proud of that skill."

Cupping her breasts with his hands, he gently squeezed. "Because it gives me access to your beautiful breasts."

He rubbed his palms against her nipples and a gentle warmth transferred from his skin to hers. The dull green glow told her the reason. "Again, Will." The light flared and a jolt travelled through her body. Will's primary power was healing, but he also had the ability to warm up a body. "I love your hands."

Releasing one breast, he lowered his head and murmured, "Good. I plan to do it often."

He took her taut nipple between his lips and sucked her deep. Fisting her hand in his hair, Petra arched her back.

God, her man had a talented tongue.

Releasing her nipple with a pop, Will stood up. Brushing his warm hands down her body and to her arse, he lifted. Petra wrapped her legs around his waist, his hard cock nestled between her thighs. She asked, "So if not the fantasy, then what?"

Will walked toward a raised table in the center of the room. Knocking the file folders on the floor, he sat her down. "I have yet to take you on this table."

Smiling, Petra wiggled against Will's hardness. He sucked in a breath and she did it again as she purred, "It's a good thing we always lock the doors now because I'm not about to let you go until you give me an orgasm."

Will cupped her face and gave a rough kiss. "I think you need more than one. After all, I need to reward you for your discovery."

She opened her lips to reply, when Will ran his hand down her thighs and put pressure on them until she released her grip. Once he was free, he sunk down.

She half-expected him to lick between her legs, but he kissed down her leg until he reached the large, gnarled scar on the front of her shin; a stark reminder of the break that had left her with a limp.

Pressing his lips to the scar, he lingered for a few seconds before raising his head. He whispered, "You are beautiful just the way you are."

Emotion choked her throat. "Will."

"I'm just being honest." Running his hands slowly up her thighs, he was soon eye level with her core.

One second passed and then another. All Will did was stare, which sent a rush of wetness between her legs.

Impatient, Petra was about to lower her hand to her clit when Will moved forward and licked her slit. Moving her hands behind her, Petra arched to the ministrations of his tongue. Each lap caused her skin to tighten and warm.

With a flick against her bundle of nerves, Petra moaned.

Sucking her tight bud hard, Petra closed her eyes. The pressure was building. Just a few more licks...

Will pulled away.

Snapping her eyes open, Petra met his gaze. "I was close, Will."

151

He took his erection into his hand and stroked slowly up and down. Petra's gaze zeroed in on the action. She couldn't help but notice the tip glistening.

Will's husky voice filled the room. "I want your first orgasm on that table to come because of my cock."

Licking her lips, Petra met his eyes again. "Then what are you waiting for?"

Will rushed forward, encircled her wrists and held her hands behind her back with one hand. With the other, he slapped his dick against her swollen flesh. "I know you like both gentle and rough. But right now, I want to take you hard."

Petra placed her feet on the table. With her knees up, she widened her legs. "Then take me, Will."

Will lowered his head and kissed the corner of her mouth. "I love you, Petra Brandt, for so many reasons." He kissed the other side. "But I think I love you most for accepting me, faults and all."

Before she could do more than open her mouth, Will thrust into her core and she cried out in pleasure.

Will took her lips in a rough kiss and swiped his tongue between hers. With her arms trapped behind her, she was at the mercy of Will's kiss, his light caress of her breast, and his cock between her thighs.

Yet he didn't move his hips, so Petra wiggled hers. Growling in her mouth, Will pulled out and pounded back in. He repeated the action, each thrust increasing his pace.

He broke the kiss to command, "Keep your hands behind your back," before releasing them and taking a better grip on her waist.

Never breaking eye contact, Petra's breasts bounced in time with Will's hips. The love, heat, and intelligence in his eyes caused warmth to flood her body and touch her heart.

If she had any say in the matter, Petra was going to keep him for the rest of her life. How she'd nearly given him up, she couldn't understand.

Will growled. "I love your brain, but stop thinking right now."

"Maybe I just want to make you work for it."

Keeping one hand on her hips, he moved the other to her clit and flicked. Still sensitive from his mouth earlier, Petra sucked in a breath. As he stroked again, Will murmured, "Now I have your attention."

She opened her mouth to reply, but Will pinched her tight bud and Petra moaned. The dual stimulation on her clit and between her thighs felt delicious, causing heat and pressure to fill her body.

Will pressed his thumb hard and it sent her over the edge. Lights flickered behind her eyes at the same time she grabbed and released Will's cock.

A few second later, Will stilled and roared as he came, the sound echoing in the room.

When he finally slumped forward and drew her body close, Petra wrapped her arms around him. Snuggling against his chest, she was content to listen to the rhythm of his breathing and his heartbeat. The sounds reminding her she was loved.

Sometime later, Will kissed the top of her head and broke the silence. "Petra Brandt, will you marry me?"

Her heart skipped a beat. After a second of shock, she pulled back to meet Will's eyes. "Yes."

He grinned. "Maybe I should add a caveat—will you marry me and promise not to fake your death to run from a drug lord?"

She grunted. "That's hardly romantic, William."

Laughing, he cupped her cheek. "But it's the truth. Never hide things from me again, Petra."

153

She softened at the fierceness in his eyes. "Never."

"Then kiss me, woman, to seal the deal."

She brought his lips down to hers. As they kissed slowly, savoring each flick and swipe, Petra could barely believe she had found her happy ending after all. Despite years of heartbreak, fear, and anger, she and Will had found one another again. It was as if they were meant to be together, no matter what happened.

Dear Reader:

Thanks for reading *Flare of Promise*. Will and Petra's story wasn't an easy one to write since I had to tie up so many loose ends, but I hope you enjoyed it. Feel free to leave a review if you did. ☺

The next book in the AMT series should be longer than this one and will be about one of the Talents (either the Earth Talent or the Wind Talent). We'll also learn a lot more about the Collector. My goal is to get it out sometime in 2017, but I don't have any more details than that right now. (The AMT books take me a lot longer to write than my other series!) You can always sign up for my newsletter at jessiedonovan.com for the latest information.

In the meantime, turn the page for an excerpt from one of my other series, the Lochguard Highland Dragons.

With Gratitude,
Jessie Donovan

The Dragon's Dilemma
(Lochguard Highland Dragons #1)

In order to pay for her father's life-saving cancer treatment, Holly Anderson offers herself up as a sacrifice and sells the vial of dragon's blood. In return, she will try to bear a Scottish dragon-shifter a child. While the dragonman assigned to her is kind, Holly can't stop looking at his twin brother. It's going to take everything she has to sleep with her assigned dragonman. If she breaks the sacrifice contract and follows her heart, she'll go to jail and not be able to take care of her father.

Even though he's not ready to settle down, Fraser MacKenzie supports his twin brother's choice to take a female sacrifice to help repopulate the clan. Yet as Fraser gets to know the lass, his dragon starts demanding something he can't have—his brother's sacrifice.

Holly and Fraser fight the pull between them, but one nearly stolen kiss will change everything. Will they risk breaking the law and betraying Fraser's twin? Or, will they find a way out of the sacrifice contract and live their own happily ever after?

Excerpt from ***The Dragon's Dilemma*** (**Lochguard Highland Dragons #1**)

CHAPTER ONE

Holly Anderson paid the taxi driver and turned toward the large stone and metal gates behind her. Looking up, she saw "Lochguard" spelled out in twisting metal, as well as some words written in a language she couldn't read.

The strange words only reminded her of where she was standing—at the entrance to the Scottish dragon-shifter clan lands.

Taking a deep breath, Holly willed her stomach to settle. She'd signed up for this. In exchange for trying to conceive a dragon-shifter's child, Clan Lochguard had given her a vial of dragon's blood. The money from the sale of that dragon's blood was funding her father's experimental cancer treatments.

All she had to do was spend the next six months sleeping with a dragon-shifter. If she didn't conceive, she could go home. If she did, then she would stay until the baby was born.

What was a minimum of six months of her life if it meant her father could live?

That's if you don't die giving birth to a half-dragon-shifter baby.

Readjusting the grip on her suitcase, Holly pushed aside the possibility. From everything she'd read, great scientific strides were being made when it came to the role dragon hormones played on a human's body. If she were lucky, there might even be a way to prevent her from dying in nine to fifteen months' time, depending on the date of conception.

This isn't work. Stop thinking about conception dates and birthing babies. After all, she might luck out and never conceive at all.

Holly moved toward the front entrance and took in the view of the loch off to the side. The dull color of the lake's surface was calm, with rugged hills and mountains framing it. Considering she was in the Scottish Highlands in November, she was just grateful that it wasn't raining.

She wondered if it was raining back in Aberdeen.

Thinking of home and her father brought tears to her eyes. He was recovering well from his first course of cancer treatments, but her father's health could decline at any moment. If only dragon's blood could cure cancer, then she wouldn't have to worry.

But since cancer was one of the illnesses dragon's blood couldn't cure, surely the Department of Dragon Affairs would grant her another few weeks to help take care of her father if she asked.

As the taxi backed down the drive, Holly turned around and flagged for the driver to come back. However, before she could barely raise a hand, a voice boomed from the right. "Lass, over here."

She turned toward the voice and a tall, blond man waved her over with a smile.

Between his wind-tousled hair, twinkling eyes, and his grin, the man was gorgeous.

Not only that, he'd distracted her from doing something daft. If Holly ran away before finishing her contract, she'd end up in jail. And then who would take care of her father?

The man motioned again. "Come, lass. I won't bite."

When he winked, some of Holly's nervousness faded. Despite the rumors of dragon-shifters being monsters, she'd followed the news stories over the last year and knew Lochguard was one of the good dragon clans. Rumors even said the Lochguard dragons and the local humans had once set up their

160

own sacrifice system long before the British government had implemented one nationwide.

It was time to experience the dragon-shifters firsthand and learn the truth.

Pushing her shoulders back, Holly put on her take no-crap nurse expression and walked over to the dragonman. When she was close enough, she asked, "Who are you?"

The man grinned wider. "I'm glad to see you're not afraid of me, lass. That makes all of this a lot easier."

Before she could stop herself, Holly blurted, "Are you really a dragon-shifter?"

The dragonman laughed. "Aye, I am. I'm the clan leader, in fact. The name's Finn. What's yours?"

The easygoing man didn't match the gruff picture she'd conjured up inside her head over the past few weeks.

Still, dragons liked strength, or so her Department of Dragon Affairs counselor had advised her. Her past decade spent as a maternity nurse would serve her well—if she could handle frantic fathers and mothers during labor, she could handle anything. "You're not a very good clan leader if you don't know my name."

Finn chuckled. "I was trying to be polite, Holly." He lowered his voice to a whisper. "Some say we're monsters that eat bairns for breakfast. I was just trying to assure you we can be friendly."

Confident the smiling man wouldn't hurt her for questioning him, she stated, "You could be acting."

"I think my mate is going to like you."

At the mention of the word "mate," Holly's confidence slipped a fraction. After all, she'd soon be having sex with a dragon-shifter to try to conceive a child. That was the price all sacrifices had to pay.

And there was always a small chance she turned out to be the dragon-shifter's true mate. If that happened, she might never be able to see her father again. Dragons were notoriously possessive. She didn't think they'd let a mate go once they found one.

Finn's voice interrupted her thoughts. "Let me take that suitcase, Holly. The sooner we get you to my place, the sooner we can settle you in and answer some of your questions."

Finn put out a hand and she passed the case over. She murmured, "Thank you."

"Considering that you're helping my clan more than you know, the least I can do is carry a bag."

She eyed the tall dragonman. "You don't have to comfort me. I know what I volunteered to do."

Finn raised a blond eyebrow. "You looked about ready to bolt or cry a few minutes ago. I think a little kindness wouldn't hurt."

He was right, not that she would admit to it. After all, she was supposed to be strong.

Holly motioned toward the gates. "How about we go so you can give me the spiel and then let me meet my dragonman?"

The dragonman's smile faded. "So you're giving orders to me now, aye?"

Even though Holly was human, she still sensed the dominance and strength in his voice. She could apologize and try to hide her true self, but that would be too tiring to keep up long term. Instead, she tilted her head. "I'm used to giving orders. In my experience, as soon as a woman goes into labor, her other half goes crazy. If I don't take charge, it could put the mother's life as well as the child's in danger. I'm sure you've read my file and should know what to expect."

The corner of Finn's mouth ticked up. "Aye, I have. But I like to test the waters with potential clan members."

"I'm not—"

Finn cut her off. "Give it time, lass. You may well become one in the long run."

Without another word, Finn started walking. Since he was at least eight inches taller than her, she had to half-jog to catch up to him. However, before she could reply, another tall, muscled dragonman approached. He still had the soft face of late adolescence and couldn't be more than twenty.

The younger dragon-shifter motioned a thumb behind him. "Archie and Cal are at it again. If you don't break it up, they might shift and start dropping each other's cattle for the second time this week."

Finn sighed. "I should assign them a full-time babysitter."

The younger man grinned. "You tried that, but my grandfather escaped, as you'll remember."

"That's because he's a sneaky bastard." Finn looked to Holly. "This is Jamie MacAllister. He'll take you to my mate, Arabella. She can help you get settled before you meet Fergus."

"Who's Fergus?" Holly asked, even though she had a feeling she knew.

Finn answered, "Fergus MacKenzie is my cousin, but he's also your assigned dragonman."

Of course she'd be given the cousin of the clan leader. After all, Holly was the first human sacrifice on Lochguard in over a decade. They'd want to keep tabs on her.

Holly didn't like it, but since she had yet to meet this Fergus, she wouldn't judge him beforehand. For all she knew, Fergus MacKenzie might be a shy, quiet copy of his cousin.

Maybe.

Not sure what else to do, Holly nodded. After giving a few more orders, Finn left to address the problem and Jamie smiled down at her. "There's never a dull moment here, lass. Welcome to Lochguard."

Holly wasn't sure if that was a warning or a welcome.

~~~

Fraser MacKenzie watched his twin brother from the kitchen. His brother, Fergus, was due to meet his human sacrifice in the next few hours and instead of celebrating his last hours of freedom, Fergus was doing paperwork.

Sometimes, Fraser wondered how they were related at all.

Taking aim, he lobbed an ice cube across the room. It bounced off his brother's cheek and Fraser shouted, "Goal."

Frowning, Fergus glanced over. "Don't you have a hole to dig? Or, maybe, some nails to pound?"

Fraser shrugged a shoulder and inched his fingers toward another ice cube. "I finished work early. After all, it's not every day your twin meets the possible mother of his child."

As Fraser picked up his second ice cube, his mother's voice boomed from behind him. "Put it down, Fraser Moore MacKenzie. I won't have you breaking something if you miss."

He looked at his mother and raised his brows. "I never miss."

Clicking her tongue, his mother, Lorna, moved toward the refrigerator. "Stop lying to me, lad. You missed a step and now have the scar near your eye to prove it."

Fraser resisted the urge to touch his scar. "That was because my sister distracted me." He placed a hand over his heart. "I was just looking out for the wee lass."

Lorna rolled her eyes. "Faye was sixteen at the time and you were too busy glaring at one of the males."

"He was trouble. Faye deserved better," Fraser replied.

Fergus looked up from his paperwork. "Where is Faye?"

Lorna waved a hand. "The same as every day. She leaves early in the morning and I don't see her again until evening."

Fraser sobered up. "I wish she'd let us help her. Does anyone know if she can fly again yet?"

His younger sister, Faye, had been shot out of the sky by an electrical blast nearly two months earlier while in dragon form and her wing had been severely damaged. While she was no longer in a wheelchair, the doctors weren't sure if Faye would ever fly again.

His mother turned toward him. "I trust Arabella to help her. Faye will come to us when she's ready."

Jumping on the chance to lighten the mood again, Fraser tossed the ice cube into the sink and added, "I'm more worried about Fergus right now anyway. Who spends their last few hours of freedom cooped up inside? Even if he doesn't want to go drinking, he could at least go for a flight."

Fergus lifted the papers in his hand. "For your information, this is all of the new procedures and suggestions from the Department of Dragon Affairs. Finn worked hard to make Lochguard one of the trial clans for these new rules, and I'm not about to fuck it up." Lorna clicked her tongue and Fergus added, "Sorry, Mum."

Lorna leaned against the kitchen counter. "I still applaud you for what you're doing, Fergus. After the last fifteen years of near-isolation, the clan desperately needs some new blood."

Fergus shrugged a shoulder. "It's not a guarantee. Besides, how could I pass up the chance to help our cousin?"

Fraser rolled his eyes. "Right, you're being all noble when I know for a fact you just want to, er," he looked to his mum and back to Fergus, "sleep with a human lass."

"No one around here has stirred a mate-claim frenzy and I'm not about to look in the other clans. I'm needed here," Fergus replied. "A human sacrifice is my only other chance."

"And what if she's not your true mate, brother? Then what?" Fraser asked.

"I'll still try to win her over. If she gives me a child, I want to try to convince the human to stay."

Lorna spoke up. "Her father's ill, Fergus. Let's see how things go before you start planning the human's future." Lorna looked to Fraser. "Let's just hope she has spirit. I can handle anything but fear."

Fraser answered, "If Finn picked her out, then we should trust that he chose a good one."

"You're right, son," Lorna answered. She waved toward the living room. "Now, go get that ice cube."

"Fergus is closer. He could just toss it over."

Fergus looked back at his stack of papers. "Get it yourself."

With a sigh, Fraser moved toward the living room. "You were always a lazy sod."

Fergus looked up. "Takes one to know one. But at least this lazy sod is about to get his own cottage."

Lorna's voice drifted into the living room. "It's about time. One down, two more to go."

Fraser scooped up the ice cube and faced his mother. "Don't worry, Mum. You'll always have me. If I'm lucky, I won't have a mate until I'm fifty."

Fergus chimed in. "She'll kick you out on your arse before then."

"I'm feeling the love, brother."

Fergus looked up with a grin. "Someone has to love you, you unlovable bastard."

Tossing the ice cube into the sink, Fraser dried his hands. "You know you'll miss me, Fergus. I give it a week and then you'll be begging for my company."

"We'll see, Fraser. If I'm lucky, I'll be spending a week in my sacrifice's bed."

The thought of not seeing his twin every day did something strange to his heart. Brushing past it, Fraser headed toward the door. "As much as I'd love to stay and watch you read boring protocol, I'm going to watch some paint dry instead."

Fergus raised an auburn eyebrow. "What happened to spending time with your brother?"

"I never said anything about spending time with you. I wanted to show you a good time. The offer's still open if you're interested."

Shaking his head, Fergus answered, "Your good times always result in us waking up in strange places and not remembering the night before. I think I'll stay here."

Fraser shrugged. "Your loss." He looked to his mum. "I'll be home for dinner, don't worry."

Lorna answered. "You'd better be. Finn wants us to have a quiet dinner with Holly and help ease her into her new life here."

"Quiet is a bit of a stretch."

Lorna picked up an apple and tossed it at his head. Once he caught it, she answered, "Just get your arse home on time."

Fraser winked. "I'll try my best, but you know how the lasses love me."

Not wanting to hear his mother's lecture about settling down for the hundredth time, Fraser ducked out the front door.

While the human wouldn't be over to their house until dinnertime, she was due to arrive on Lochguard at any moment.

He had known that Fergus wouldn't want to go out, but asking gave Fraser the perfect cover and no one would suspect what he was about to do.

It was time to spy on his brother's future female and make sure she was worthy of a MacKenzie.

———————

Want to read the rest?
The Dragon's Dilemma is available in paperback

For exclusive content and updates, sign up for my newsletter at:

http://www.jessiedonovan.com

Author's Note

My first three AMT books were my first ever books I published. If you've been with me from the beginning and waited the nearly two years between *Shadow of Temptation* and *Flare of Promise*, I thank you from the bottom of my heart. As much as I enjoy the challenge of the AMT books, they don't earn me very much money. I write because I love it, but I also have to pay my bills. But now that I have enough books out in my dragon series to pay the bills, I sometimes have the opportunity to just write. *Flare of Promise* is one of those stories. :) I will eventually finish the AMT series, but it will take some time to get there. I hope you can be patient!

Besides my readers, I also have my cover artist, Clarissa Yeo of Yocla Designs, and my editor, Becky Johnson of Hot Tree Editing, to thank. I couldn't imagine writing without either of those two fabulous ladies! I also have some awesome and invaluable beta readers: Donna H. Iliana G, and Alyson S.

The world of the Four Talents will really be gearing up in the next book. Between the curse, James Sinclair, and the Collector, poor Neena is going to be working overtime…

Thanks so much for reading! If you wish to stay up-to-date on new releases as well as receive information, exclusive excerpts, and reveals, make sure to sign up for my newsletter at jessiedonovan.com

About the Author

Jessie Donovan wrote her first story at age five, and after discovering *The Dragonriders of Pern* series by Anne McCaffrey in junior high, she realized people actually wanted to read stories like those floating around inside her head. From there on out, she was determined to tap into her over-active imagination and write a book someday.

After living abroad for five years and earning degrees in Japanese, Anthropology, and Secondary Education, she buckled down and finally wrote her first full-length book. While that story will never see the light of day, it laid the world-building groundwork of what would become her debut paranormal romance, *Blaze of Secrets*.

Jessie loves to interact with readers, and when not traipsing around some foreign country on a shoestring, can often be found on Facebook:

http://www.facebook.com/JessieDonovanAuthor

And don't forget to sign-up for her newsletter to receive sneak peeks and inside information. You can sign-up on her website:

http:///www.jessiedonovan.com

Printed in Poland
by Amazon Fulfillment
Poland Sp. z o.o., Wrocław